Crime in the Community

Cecilia Peartree

Copyright © 2015 Cecilia Peartree
All rights reserved.
ISBN: 1477506381
ISBN-13: 978-1477506387

CRIME IN THE COMMUNITY

Chapter 1 Petunias

All hell broke loose in the next street.

Amaryllis took a moment to swear silently and comprehensively before setting off at a run towards the source of the disturbance, wresting the gun from her shoulder holster as she did so.

She dived down a lane between two houses, accelerating into the darkness, and ran full tilt into someone coming the other way. She yelped – and was silenced by a large hand slapped over her mouth. Another hand chopped the gun out of her grasp and before she could do anything her arms were pinned behind her. She struggled instinctively, trying to get her tired brain to come up with an escape plan. Her captor dragged her in the direction of the action. They walked from the darkness into the flickering light of the flames.

'Hey!' he yelled in a deep voice that carried above the sounds of crackling, wailing, screaming and the rest.

It was hard to make sense of what was going on, but Amaryllis saw a few random figures in the smoke – figures in and out of uniform: some of them standing still, apparently too stunned to do anything, others staggering around as if injured, while a few people had recovered quickly and were helping the rest to safety. The uniforms were British army. Amaryllis and her colleagues had been tipped off that something was about to happen, but they had been too late to prevent it.

'Hey, English!' shouted her captor. 'I have one of yours – do you want her?'

Two figures emerged from the smoke. They stopped short. At first Amaryllis thought her captor was holding a gun on them, but, twisting in his grasp to look at him in the firelight, she realised that he had explosives packed round his body. 'Nice,' she thought, and realised she had said it aloud.

Nobody was going to rescue her at the risk of blowing everyone else up. She sighed. She was going to have to do it herself again as usual.

In this region men didn't expect women to put up much of a resistance, which was one thing in her favour. Another thing was that she had come top of her class in spy school when it came to working with explosives. And the third, decisive thing was that she had a syringe in her pocket containing a drug which, if only she could use it, would put her captor to sleep for a very long time – perhaps not long enough for a prickly hedge to grow up round him, but near enough.

Before the others even had time to recall their hostage situation training, she had wrenched one hand free, hooked a finger round the trigger mechanism he held, disabled it in one practised movement , extracted the syringe from her pocket and used it. She had seen the man slump to his knees without even knowing anything had hit him, and she had decided to retire.

It was just too boring and predictable being a spy. She would retire and grow petunias in a window-box.

She would retire and take up knitting, embroidery and pigeon breeding.

She would retire to a small community and provide nibbles for church socials.

~~~

For once even Christopher was satisfied with the range of nibbles on offer at the regular monthly meeting of the Pitkirtly Local Improvement Forum in the village pub, the Queen of Scots. There were cocktail sausages, samosas, carrot sticks and Pringles, and he had even caught a glimpse of two different varieties of dip at the other end of the bar. He took this as a sign that western civilization had finally arrived in Pitkirtly. The Queen of Scots wasn't exactly a cosmopolitan wine bar, but it was undoubtedly the nearest thing this side of the Forth Bridge.

He had just stuffed a handful of Pringles in his mouth when the door of the bar swung open. All eyes, including Christopher's, swerved to look in that direction, and stayed swerved. A tall red-haired figure clad in deep purple stood in the doorway for a moment before walking lithely forward into the room. The door clicked shut behind her. An unusual - and uneasy - silence spread through the room, wafting across people's heads rather like the veil of smoke that had, in less enlightened times but still within Christopher's memory span, emerged from Jock McLean's pipe in these very premises.

Women were certainly allowed into the lounge bar of the Queen of Scots, in fact some would say the provision of tables and chairs actively encouraged them to come in. But Christopher knew that once ensconced they were expected to know their place, which was in the corner, wearing a woolly hat at all times regardless of the ambient temperature, and drinking a womanly drink such as Dubonnet and lemonade while not drawing attention to themselves in any way. However, there was still instinctive resistance to women with an aura of ownership of self and surroundings, who walked decisively up to the bar and ordered whisky and water, without the tiniest hesitation on the threshold to try and judge whether the atmosphere was hostile or welcoming.

And as for walking smoothly and lithely over to the chairman's table and speaking directly to him before the meeting even reached an appropriate hiatus -

'Is this the monthly meeting of the Pitkirtly Local Improvement Forum? PLIF?' enquired the intruder.

Christopher nodded.

'So, who exactly is part of the forum?' the red-haired newcomer pressed him. 'Is it everybody in the pub, or just the select few?'

'The meetings are open to everybody who lives in Pitkirtly,' said Christopher. 'But there's a steering group - I'm the chair at the moment.'

And had been the chair since the beginning of time, he didn't add. If she hung around for long enough, she would work it out for herself.

'I'm sorry,' he added, 'we're in the middle of an agenda item - you'll have to wait until we've finished and then raise whatever you want to say under AOCB.'

'Fine,' she said, sitting down at the next table with the air of someone who knew exactly what she wanted and was willing to wait indefinitely for it. Her hair stood up attentively in dark red spikes.

'So,' said Christopher, raising his voice. 'The next item - the allotments by the roadworks on the A90. Jock - you were looking into an application under the Sites of Special Scientific Interest scheme.'

'Bad news, I'm afraid, Chris,' said Jock, beaming with satisfaction. 'The scheme's past its closing date for this year.'

'I'm not very pleased about that, Jock. In fact, I'm seriously displeased. I understood we had plenty of time to apply.'

'We would have done, Chris.' Jock nodded politely towards the newcomer in a way that made Christopher, who had always hated being called Chris, want even more than ever to wring his neck. 'We would've done. But with me going to Canada for three weeks, there was an unavoidable delay....'

'Last year it was Thailand,' grumbled Christopher. 'Are you ever in this country for more than two weeks at a time?'

'I can only do what I can do,' said Jock. 'If you don't want me to get involved, fine. I've got plenty of other fish to fry.'

He stomped out of the bar.

'Are you short of a quorum now?' enquired the annoying woman. 'I could stand in.'

'No, we're not short of a quorum!' snapped Christopher. 'He's only off for a smoke.'

There was silence at the two tables, and a babble of inconsequential conversation from the rest of the bar. Actually, Christopher reflected crossly, not relishing the idea of 'his' organisation being scrutinised under the microscope of an outsider's gaze, the content of the meetings was often fairly inconsequential too.

'Is it time for AOCB yet?' asked the interloper.

Christopher resisted the urge to put his head in his hands.

'We can't proceed until Jock comes back.'

'Do you organise events too?'

'Events?'

'Do you have a fund-raising team?'

'Not exactly - no.'

'I suppose you have a constitution, and all the requisite policies in place.'

'Are you from the Cooncil or what?'

Big Dave spoke up at last. He had got to his feet and was now towering over the woman, making her appear almost fragile by comparison.

'The Cooncil? Goodness, no. What an awful thought.'

She smiled to herself at the absurdity of it.

Christopher decided he quite liked her sleek style and the way she refused to acknowledge Big Dave's size and menacing tone.

'I'm Christopher Wilson, chair,' he said, standing up and extending a hand towards her. She ignored it.

'Amaryllis Peebles. I've never been on a committee before.'

'You aren't on one now, hen,' said Big Dave.

'Ah, but I live in Pitkirtly, so I plan to attend the meetings.'

'You live here?' asked Christopher, surprised. Most of the inhabitants of Pitkirtly were only there because their fathers, mothers, grandmothers and so on had lived there, and they couldn't think of anywhere else to go. The others - the ones in the new houses in Upper Pitkirtly - spent all their time and energy commuting into Edinburgh to work and so fortunately had nothing left for community activities, although Christopher had been living in fear for a while that they would decide to infiltrate PLIF and would take it over and insist something was actually done about improving the local area. He didn't think Amaryllis fitted into either of the categories. Or, as far as he could tell, any category.

'I've retired here,' said Amaryllis, obviously lying through her very even white teeth, since she didn't look a day over forty. Well, it was hard to tell how old she was.

10

Any age between twenty-three and sixty-five, was Christopher's guess, and he wouldn't have dared to put anything that specific into words.

'OK,' said Christopher, 'fine. Now, the next item on the agenda - '

Jock McLean burst back in at this point, breathless and indignant.

'It's raining,' he complained at first, and then, in a doom-laden voice, 'and there's a lad from the Council coming down the street.'

'How do you know he's from the Council?' said Christopher. 'Does he have a name badge? A big banner?'

'A swag bag labelled 'expenses'?' added Big Dave, chortling.

'A scruffy leather jacket and jeans and a silly wee beard,' said Jock, nodding. 'A look of the sixties about him.'

There was a collective groan. Christopher shifted slightly in his chair to try and conceal the scruffy leather jacket that was hanging on the back of it.

'Maybe he's come to check the road surface,' said Christopher hopefully.

The sky was darkening outside in an ominous way, and just as the door of the bar swung open again there was a portentous roll of thunder with the accompanying sound of massed raindrops landing on the pavement. The man with the silly wee beard and the look of the sixties about him made his entrance. He had a bland face which was at the moment fixed, as far as could be determined under the beard, in a painful-looking pleasant smile. He went to the bar, running the gauntlet of a group of regulars, who gawped at him, no doubt wondering which of them had fallen foul of the local authorities.

After getting his half pint, the man swivelled round in mid-sip, perhaps trying to catch as many people's eyes as possible before his question.

'Is this the regular monthly meeting of PLIF?' he asked.

Everyone looked at Christopher.

'Yes,' he said, trying not to sound too self-important. 'Can I help you? Are you a local resident?'

'Just down the road,' said the man. 'Aberdour.'

'The meeting's open to anyone who lives in Pitkirtly,' said Christopher.

'I'm here on behalf of the Community Development and Knowledge department. Of the Council.'

'Community Development and Knowledge? I thought it was Social Work and Communities.'

'We've merged with the old Communities and Schools department,' the man explained. 'Everything's been re-jigged. So you'll be getting your funding through us in future.' He paused ominously. 'That is, of course, if you satisfy our criteria.' Another pause. 'But that shouldn't be a problem, of course.'

'Shouldn't it?' said Christopher, baffled by the mention of funding.

'As long as you can tick all the right boxes.'

'Boxes?' said Christopher even more helplessly.

'Do you want me to throw him out?' said Big Dave, giving the man one of his glares.

'I don't think that'll be necessary,' said Christopher. 'So what were you saying about those boxes?'

'Just carry on with your meeting,' said the man. 'I'll observe, if I may?'

'Right,' said Christopher doubtfully.

The man held out a hand suddenly.

'Steve Paxman.'

'I'm Christopher Wilson... you can sit round at this side if you like.... I'll take AOCB next.'

There was a silence - as there often was at this point in the proceedings.

'Any other business at all?' said Christopher, by now desperate for anything that would delay the evil moment when he would have to go home and see what sort of state Caroline was in and judge what kind of damage limitation might be necessary.

Amaryllis Peebles coughed quietly.

'Yes?' he said, not expecting very much.

'I wondered if you had ever looked for premises of your own.'

'Premises?' he said blankly.

'Yes,' she nodded. 'Premises where you could carry out your primary aim of improving Pitkirtly. Without being interrupted. By anybody.'

She seemed to be looking meaningfully at Steve Paxman as she said it, but it was impossible for Christopher to tell what was in her mind. Her expression was cool and calm, her speech quiet and rational. It was a novelty in a woman.

'Well - I don't know,' said Christopher.

'What's wrong with the pub?' growled Big Dave.

'Did you have anywhere in mind?' enquired Christopher. 'There aren't that many suitable places in Pitkirtly - in fact, I don't think I can think of any, off the top of my head. Well, that's why we meet here, you see.'

'That and the drinks,' said Jock McLean, laughing. Christopher willed him to shut up. Steve Paxman was looking at the old fool with an expression of sympathetic interest which must surely be false. Nobody could possibly find Jock sympathetic, or in any way interesting for that matter.

'What about the village hall?' said Amaryllis smoothly.

Jaws dropped open; glasses were frozen halfway to lips; one glass was dropped on the floor.

'The village hall?' said Steve Paxman. 'That sounds like an interesting idea.'

'It isn't,' said Christopher shortly.

Silence. Christopher didn't look at anyone, especially Amaryllis. He tried not to feel ashamed of his haste in dismissing her idea. Perhaps he should be more open to new ideas; perhaps he was just being lazy about it.

'So tell me about this village hall, then,' persisted Steve.

'It isn't really –, ' said Christopher.

'It's derelict now, of course,' said Amaryllis. Christopher realised Steve had been addressing her. He raised his head, deciding it might be a good idea to watch what was going on as well as listening, in case he missed anything. He wasn't a great one for interpreting body language and nuances of speech; he had to give himself as many clues as possible.

'It's been derelict for years,' said Jock. 'They might as well tear it down and start all over again.'

'I wouldn't say that,' said Amaryllis coolly.

'Well, it's a talking point anyway,' said Steve. He looked at his watch. 'I've got to be at Ballingry at eight – maybe next time we could go and have a look at this place.'

'Next time?' said Christopher faintly.

'How about next Tuesday evening?' Steve delved into a scruffy briefcase and pulled out a scruffy filofax bulging with odd bits of paper. He made a note.

'Wednesday afternoon would be better,' said Big Dave.

'OK, Tuesday at six-thirty it is,' said Steve, scribbling. 'We'll meet at the hall, yes?'

'That would be good,' said Amaryllis.

'Any questions?' said Steve.

'No,' said Christopher. 'Thanks for coming along.'

It was only by an extreme effort of will-power that he forced the words out of his mouth. They tried to hide behind his teeth but he was ruthless. Afterwards he wondered why he had bothered.

Steve nodded at them and left.

'The iron hand in the velvet glove,' nodded Jock, sucking hard on his pipe.

'Aye,' said Big Dave. 'Never trust a man with a silly looking beard and a filofax.'

The gathering broke up after that: their innocent pleasure in taking part in being responsible enough members of the Big Society to serve on a steering group had been dented, and Christopher just wanted to be on his own to get to grips with the new situation. He unintentionally found himself walking up the road with Amaryllis. Jock McLean wasn't far behind, and could perhaps be relied upon to come to the rescue – or, on a bad day, to dig an even deeper hole for Christopher than the latter could manage on his own.

'So why do you want to get involved with the Forum?' said Christopher, sticking to a safe topic.

'The Forum - oh, PLIF, you mean? I couldn't resist the name. It was just so ridiculous... Actually, I used to live in a village at one time. It was small and cosy, everybody knew everyone else. There was a village hall with coffee mornings and whist drives. I acted in the local drama group. There was a village school with about twenty pupils. The sun shone every day and there was honey still for tea.... You know what I mean?'

'Yes, I think so,' said Christopher. Strictly speaking he was only familiar with that kind of village through watching 'Miss Marple' and 'Midsomer Murders' on television, but he felt the two programmes pretty much covered the whole village scenario.

'A bit like Miss Marple,' said Amaryllis. 'Or Midsomer Murders.'

'Ah,' said Christopher.

'Anyway, when I found out about the village hall here, I thought it would be nice to try and get it on its feet again. As a sort of community centre.'

There were a few phrases that struck terror into Christopher, and 'community centre' was one of them. For some reason he thought of them as places where old people played Bingo in the afternoons, with nothing to offer anyone under sixty-seven unless they had a small child who went to a playgroup. The fact that he had spent quite a lot of time a couple of years before trying to persuade his aged father to go along to a carpet bowls session at an old people's day centre, only for Dad to die on that very carpet on his first visit, had perhaps prejudiced him unduly.

Distracted by the memory, he stepped out to cross the road without looking, having forgotten that cars did occasionally find their way down through the maze of narrow cobbled streets, and would have been mown down by a shiny black car that appeared from nowhere if Amaryllis hadn't grabbed him by the sleeve of the scruffy leather jacket that had embarrassed him earlier, and pulled him back on to the pavement.

'Idiot!' she screeched after the black car, making a variety of gestures, some of which Christopher hadn't seen before even when Young Dave crashed his motorbike into the wheelie bin outside the Queen of Scots.

'There are quite a lot of young people in this town,' Amaryllis continued, as they stood at the edge of the pavement like children, looking right, left and right again in contravention of the Green Cross Code, 'but you never see them outdoors. It's as if there's a kind of invisible curfew, and none of them are allowed out after dark. They could be doing all kinds of things - '

'With all due respect,' interrupted Jock, who had fallen into step with them, attracted either by Amaryllis's great legs or just by the opportunity to annoy Christopher, 'I think you'll find that's what most people are afraid of, dear.'

'But that's so wrong,' said Amaryllis earnestly, which appealed to Christopher. He liked people to take things seriously. 'We should be encouraging young people to do their thing, without being overly censorious or disparaging. Art - drama - table-tennis - badminton - just hanging out with their friends - '

Jock made a strange noise through his pipe.

'I think you'll find they don't want to do any of those things,' he said. 'In my experience all kids want to do after school is go home and sit in their room playing computer games half the night. That's until they're old enough or stupid enough to want to spend all their time trying to get hold of Buckfast, and then they hang around on street corners drinking for the next few years.'

Christopher wondered vaguely why Jock had spent so many years trying to teach those very same kids if he felt like that. Or maybe it was teaching that had made him so cynical. It was an interesting chicken and egg question.

'And then there are all sorts of people who're at home during the day and could do with something to get them out of the house,' said Amaryllis, studiously ignoring Jock. 'And of course a lot of people would like to be more active in the evenings, after work, and we could run chess clubs and Scottish country dancing classes for them. And then we could organise special events to raise money for improvements....'

'We?' said Christopher. It was a shame to throw cold water on her ideas really, but he couldn't help feeling just a tiny bit miffed that she was running away with all this, as if nobody else had ever thought of doing anything of the kind before. After all, he or any of the people on the Forum could have had just as brilliant an idea as she had - and with the local knowledge to put it into practice as well.

Harsh reality cleared its throat and stepped on to the stage here, forcing Christopher to picture all the people involved, and face up to the fact that none of them would ever have come up with anything if they had sat in the Queen of Scots from now until the sea level rose however many metres it was and swept them all away to perdition.

'I'm sorry,' he said, seeing the glow recede slowly from her eyes and a dull look of acceptance start to wash in. 'I'm sorry, of course you're welcome to join the committee. We can't afford to turn anyone away who has such great ideas and such a go-ahead outlook... I'm sure we'll need your special skills if this - er - thing goes ahead.'

'I doubt if my special skills will ever be needed in Pitkirtly,' she said with an enigmatic smile, but offered him her hand to shake. 'Thanks, Christopher. I'll really work at this.'

'Just a word of gentle advice,' said Christopher, noticing that Jock had moved on ahead again, bored with the conversation already, as he usually was when kids were mentioned. 'It's best to soft-pedal a bit with people like Jock and Big Dave, if you get my drift. They're a bit set in their ways. Slow to change. You know.'

'I'll remember that,' she said.

Chapter 2 Steve's Ultimatum

It was raining again the following Tuesday, although the threatening thunder had made a tactical withdrawal for the time being, and the light wasn't good, especially under the ornamental cherry trees that seemed to close in at the sides of the road further down the hill, making the pavement slippery with their carelessly discarded blossoms. There were a few houses here, large Victorian villas with big gardens, probably built for merchants who had done unspeakable things in the East or West Indies, and now occupied by the secretive bankers and lawyers who were only glimpsed in the village if they accidentally left their car windows down when driving to or from work in Edinburgh. Christopher had never really questioned the lack of community spirit in the little town, but thinking about it now as they headed towards the old higgledy-piggledy fishermen's houses down by the river, he realised the place was divided into two or three sections, with the riverside dwellers resenting the people in the newer estates up the hill, and both resenting the inhabitants of the Victorian villas. He had a sudden twinge of guilt about not being able to bring the factions together into a coalition under the umbrella of the Forum, but as always he brushed the guilt aside, telling himself he had done all he could, and it wasn't his fault if the people around here were born awkward.

He felt self-conscious now in the scruffy old leather jacket, as if he were guilty of attempting to appear younger and more cool than he really was, although he realised it probably had the opposite effect. Nothing more embarrassing than an ageing rocker, after all. He wondered briefly whether to put on his scruffy brown tweed one instead, but decided against it. The brown tweed jacket was definitely the jacket of an archivist, and now that he was no longer a member of that profession he felt as if he wasn't entitled to wear it. Christopher had resolved a long time ago not to try to be something he wasn't – if only he could instead be proud of what he was, but that was out of the question these days. Anyway, if Amaryllis mistook him for someone young and cool that was her problem.

'It's just down here on the left,' called Amaryllis from the back of the group. 'Turn along Merchantman Wynd.'

The street was a cul de sac once notorious for its ladies of the night plying their trade in the shadows but now more famous for its award-winning mews-style town houses. This was all new to Christopher; he couldn't remember when he had last come along here, and now he stared in puzzlement at the twee balconies and incongruous Mediterranean white washed walls and brightly coloured creeping plants. How sad that some people weren't satisfied with the Scottish grey stone, off-white net curtains and statutory patch of grass that distinguished the houses in most towns along the coast.

'So tell me, ' said Steve Paxman in a pleasant tone that very nearly concealed the hint of the KGB-style interrogation techniques that were undoubtedly at his disposal. 'I'm guessing you have all the paperwork for PLIF in place - written constitution, accounts, policies. I'm sure you're the kind of person who would be meticulous about it all.'

In other areas of his life Christopher was indeed a very meticulous man, but he had considered the Forum as a red-tape-free zone, a haven where he could relax in the knowledge that nobody would ever come looking for paperwork.

'I am quite meticulous,' he admitted, playing for time and wondering all over again why exactly Steve Paxman was so interested in this small local organisation. 'But I'm not sure that I can lay my hands on every last document... not off the top of my head....'

'Turn into the yard here,' called Amaryllis, unexpectedly coming to his rescue. 'On the right - look for the orange door.'

Amaryllis's 'yard' was a wilderness surrounding a tumbledown structure - it would surely have been an exaggeration to call it a building. The faded orange door was attached to its frame by one hinge. A beech tree in the centre of the wilderness had been allowed to run wild and one of its branches now extended through a gap in a window. The tree probably supported its own eco-system. Curiously, though, Christopher noticed that even before any of them had set foot in the place the tall grass had been flattened in places and that a very rough path led through it towards the back of the structure. Vandals, he thought dismissively, or school kids. Same thing really. He immediately felt cross with himself for spending too much time with Jock McLean and absorbing his attitudes.

'Wow, what a great resource!' breathed Steve Paxman, next to him. 'Shame it's been allowed to get into this state.'

Again Christopher wondered if Steve was deliberately trying to make him feel guilty or if it was just his manner.

They headed up the path of broken paving stones towards the orange door, their footsteps accompanied by a backing track of muffled swearing as people stepped right off the slabs and got their shoes stuck in the surrounding mud. Christopher stood aside to let Steve go in first. If he was so excited about this resource, let him be the one to have his skull fractured by a piece of falling roof.

Amaryllis caught up with them. For some reason all the other Forum regulars were just as reluctant as Christopher to enter the place.

'It's safe enough inside,' she said, and somehow Steve Paxman was persuaded, without any words being exchanged, to let her go in ahead of him.

'You mean you've been in here before?' said Christopher once they stood in the large room looking up at the uneven holes in the roof, and trying to avoid the raindrops that were falling through the holes into small puddles on the floor. There was a smell of mould or of dead things inside the walls.

'I popped in the other day, yes,' said Amaryllis. She waved her arms round. 'It's got potential, hasn't it?'

'Aye, potential to be knocked down and replaced with a proper building,' said Big Dave. It was quite a long sentence by his standards, signifying that he felt particularly cynical about this expedition.

There was a general muttering of agreement. Big Dave had spoken for all of them.

They were turning to leave when Steve Paxman cleared his throat.

'This seems like a good time to voice my concerns,' he said.

Christopher couldn't have agreed less. It was completely the wrong time. There was rain trickling down people's necks, their feet were wet, they resented the time spent away from the pub on this wild-goose chase, they resented the presence of Steve and Amaryllis. He and his friends didn't ask much, just to be left alone to run their own lives without interference from the Council, who, as far as they were concerned, only existed to collect the rubbish, to keep the street lighting in a good state of repair and to run schools in order to keep kids out from under people's feet as far as possible.

'Shouldn't we go somewhere dry?' he suggested mildly.

'Oh no - I think the odd drip will wake us up and help us focus,' said Steve.

Christopher looked round at his motley crew and detected quite a lot of focussed hatred of Steve: Big Dave, of course, didn't bother to conceal his hostility, but stood behind the younger, shorter man, fists clenched and head lowered in a way that, if Steve had been able to see him, would probably have alarmed him seriously; Jock McLean lit up his pipe and held it tightly between his teeth pointing straight at Steve's jugular in a menacing way; Mrs Stevenson, one of the woolly hat brigade - what was she thinking of, coming all this way? She would be lucky to get back up the hill again with her dodgy hip and blood pressure problem - was staring witch-like at the man from the Council, and muttering what sounded suspiciously like an incantation; Young Dave, at least thirty years younger than Big Dave and a little less colossal, was standing by the doorway, possibly with intent to block it. There were a few other hangers-on still around, the ones with the shorter attention spans having retired to the pub again. Amaryllis was studying her feet with a pretence of interest. In any case it was impossible for Christopher to tell what she was thinking.

'This building belongs to the town,' said Steve unexpectedly.

'You mean the Council?' said Jock McLean.

'No,' Steve said with a sigh. 'Not to the Council – to the town of Pitkirtly itself. The original hall was paid for by the skippers of the merchant ships that berthed in the old harbour down there, and put in trust for the people of the town, along with the land it was built on. Of course, the old hall was destroyed by fire a century ago and this one here was built, I believe, in the 1950s by a local benefactor. There was a special clause in the skippers' trust to say the patch of land and any buildings on it should never be taken over by the local Council, whatever happened, but it should be kept in use for the benefit of the community.'

Christopher frowned.

'I don't remember hearing about this before. It sounds like a very odd arrangement.'

'The papers have only just surfaced. Remember the excavations in Mary King's Close?'

'That's nothing to do with us,' said Jock McLean, suspicious as ever. 'That's in Edinburgh.'

Steve Paxman sighed again.

'There was a similar excavation here soon after Mary King's Close opened to the public. In Well Street - it was thought there might have been a plague pit, which certain people were keen to market as a tourist attraction. In addition to certain other evidence too gruesome to mention here, the excavation turned up a box of old town records. Then when West Fife Council was set up after the millennium rationalisation, we took over and there was a new policy on libraries and archives.'

'I'm aware of that,' said Christopher sourly. He had been made redundant from his job in the archives at the time of this reorganisation.

'All the old local documents were transferred to us so that we could get the new archives people to look them over. The team have only just got round to it. They were busy with all the mining legacy stuff at first, but a member of the public started pestering them about this.'

Christopher stared hard at Amaryllis. Her startlingly blue eyes had an innocent expression which he suspected was completely fake. He wouldn't put it past her to pretend to be just an ordinary member of the public if she chose, although even on their short acquaintance he could tell she was anything but ordinary.

'But if it belongs to the town couldn't we – um – delegate it to the Council to look after?' Christopher blurted out.

He had warmed very slightly to Steve Paxman, who seemed far too tired and worn for a man of his age, as well as sounding genuinely interested in local history, a subject dear to Christopher as well. But the smile that Steve smiled at that moment was one of pure malice.

'Well, it would have been a possibility a few years ago,' he said smoothly. 'But we've been pursuing a policy of devolving authority to local organisations similar to yours. Well, perhaps not entirely similar,' he added, distaste making his beard curl in various directions. 'Some of my colleagues see the Local Improvement Forum as an ad hoc drinking club for which you've received –'

'Aaargh!'

'Get off!'

There was a disturbance near where Jock McLean and Young Dave were standing. It was impossible to tell who had started it, but they suddenly seemed to be trying to push each other over. They were evidently getting very restive.

'Sorry,' said Christopher to Steve Paxman. 'What were you saying?'

He hoped the two would stop squabbling for a little bit longer so that he could hear all that Steve Paxman had to say, but Young Dave had other ideas. He maneouvred himself out of Jock McLean's reach, and advanced on the man from the Council.

'I'd be careful what I say, if I were you, Mr Paxman. Be very sure of your evidence before you start hurling accusations about.'

Young Dave was a lawyer in his spare time - when he wasn't propping up the bar in the Queen of Scots, that was.

'How do you know I'm going to hurl accusations?' said Steve Paxman, eyes glittering. 'You're not in this Forum for the sake of the community, are you? It's just an excuse to meet at the pub.'

He made a harmless activity by a group of public-spirited local people sound like some sort of crime.

'We'll meet again next week,' Steve continued, 'when I'll have a proposition for you, and I will expect to see evidence of a properly constituted body and of the will to take things forward for the betterment of the community.'

He paused.

'Or else what?' said Big Dave suddenly from behind him. A normal man would have jumped out of his skin, and made a run for the door. Without even turning round, Steve Paxman said,

'It wasn't a threat. I really am expecting to see these things.'

He walked towards the doorway. Young Dave stepped aside to let him past. He went out.

Those who were left breathed a collective sigh of relief. Jock McLean relaxed the grip of his lips round the stem of his pipe so suddenly that the pipe fell on the floor, where it might have been in danger of setting fire to the worn lino had there not been so much damp around. Big Dave unclenched his fists. Christopher realised he had been holding in his stomach in sympathy, and when he relaxed, his suddenly expanded girth caused the button at the waistband of his trousers to fly off and hit Amaryllis on the elbow as she moved towards the little central group. She jumped and quickly glanced round the room.

'Aye, and you can go too,' said Big Dave to her. 'You were the one that started all this.'

'No,' she said, 'but I do have a confession to make..... I was the one that identified the village hall and researched the history of it and alerted the Council archivist, so it's my fault in a way.'

'Not just in a way!' said Jock McLean. 'It's your fault, full stop.'

'It was only a matter of time before the Council caught up with you,' she said to him. 'You couldn't expect to carry on with it indefinitely. They were bound to go through one of their phases of tightening up on community organisations at some point.'

'But we're such small fry,' Christopher blurted out.

The others all looked at him accusingly.

'I mean,' he added, 'why are they bothering about us? We don't have to answer to them and they have so many other problems.'

'Hmph!' said Big Dave. 'Problems! They don't know the meaning of the word.'

'That's exactly why they're bothering about you,' said Amaryllis. 'You're small and can be brought under control - they think. The other problems are too big to be solved - traffic congestion, how to sell a tramline along the coast, why schools aren't working....'

'That last one's easy enough,' grunted Jock McLean, who had once been a teacher. 'Get the politicians to stop interfering in them.'

'Well, anyway,' said Christopher, 'what are we going to do about it?'

'If I'm going to be mulling over large complex issues that don't have any solution,' said Big Dave solemnly, 'I'm going to need a drink. Let's get back to the Queen of Scots and work out how to fix that smarmy bastard.'

'Fine by me,' said Jock.

Without any further discussion they all trooped out of the place again - it really wasn't fit to be called a building - and set off up the hill. Christopher, although he had done his best to avoid speaking to her, found himself walking alongside Amaryllis. He glanced at her furtively when he thought she wasn't looking, wondering if he had imagined the lithe figure and stunning legs. How old was she exactly?

He didn't ask.

'Seen enough?' she enquired. He didn't think she was annoyed but it was hard to be sure.

'Amaryllis, please don't take this the wrong way, but what are you doing here?'

'I told you, I've retired here.... I like it here. It's small and simple and - safe.'

'Safe?' Christopher was startled. Of all the qualities he might have expected Amaryllis to prize in a town - if he had even had time to think about it - safety certainly wasn't one of them.

29

'Well, maybe that was a bad choice of words,' she said. 'Secure - as if nothing ever changes.'

'Yes,' he said, drawing the word out into a couple of syllables. He had a feeling, based on nothing, that her first choice of words had been a more accurate statement of her reasons. But he knew better than to pursue that. If she chose to confide in him later on, that was her own look-out. He gave himself a mental shake. It felt as if something in his brain had been jolted out of position by today's events, and he would have to try and get himself re-aligned. Mental Pilates, that was the thing. If only somebody would invent it.

Christopher had a brainwave. It didn't happen very often, but he knew that one of his own special skills was to recognise the moment when it did, and act on it.

'Why don't we have a sub-committee?' he said excitedly. The excitement was caused mainly by his surprise at having had an idea at all. 'A building sub-committee - to deal with aspects of the old village hall building. Then it can just report back to the main steering group and not too many people will have to get to grips with the fine detail of your - er - very interesting ideas.'

'A sub-committee? Are you sure you're not just trying to shelve this?' she asked sharply.

'No of course not - it's a way of making progress without getting bogged down in general discussions about whose round it is and whether Mrs McDougal should be allowed to take on another allotment.'

'My goodness,' she said. 'It's as exciting as that, is it?'

'Even more exciting sometimes,' he said darkly.

They had reached the exterior of the Queen of Scots. He knew the others would be waiting for him inside, ready to dissect what had happened, to mull over its implications, as well as the many attributes of Amaryllis and probably the entire history of the town to date. Christopher felt very tired. He sensed that everything was about to change, and his mind was already starting to man the barricades.

A fair-haired man in a grey suit stood by the door. He looked at them for longer than seemed natural. Christopher decided he probably fancied Amaryllis.

'Well, must be getting on home, or I won't see the kids before they go to bed,' he said to Amaryllis.

'Kids? Well, goodbye then. See you around,' she said.

He suddenly realised what he had said.

'It isn't what you think,' he said.

Her smile was sad.

'It never is.'

Chapter 3 Building a Community Strategy and other Stories

'You're all taking a big step forward in deciding to build a community strategy, and I want you to give yourselves a huge round of applause,' said Steve Paxman, leaning over the conference table in the big impersonal meeting room he had hired at the Holiday Inn Pitkirtly. Christopher had never set foot in the place before, although his sister Caroline was a member of the health club here and visited at least once every six months to get value for money out of her three hundred pounds a year subscription.

There was a stunned silence from the members of PLIF, most of whom, as Christopher was well aware, had not suspected themselves of deciding to build a community strategy. Young Dave poured a glass of water and sipped at it, while Mrs Stevenson stared out of the window at the view of the tarmac car park outside or perhaps at the Lomond Hills in the distance.

'We don't do that kind of thing here, Mr Paxman,' said Big Dave.

'Come on, Davie, I thought I asked you to call me Steve. We're all on the same side, after all.'

'Stalin was on the same side as us once,' said Big Dave, tactful as ever. 'And it's Dave, not Davie. Davie's a diminutive and I find it patronising and insulting.'

'I'm sorry, Dave,' said Steve, floundering a bit but making a reasonable recovery. 'So - let's get on with building the strategy then!'

To Christopher's ears it sounded much the same as 'let's all jump out of an aeroplane, then' or even 'let's all go and jump off a cliff like the lemmings we are', except that he was sure he had read recently that lemmings didn't really jump off cliffs. Jock McLean sucked on his empty pipe, daring Steve to invoke the non-smoking policy of the hotel, and glared alternately at Christopher, whom he blamed, somewhat unfairly, for starting the whole thing, and Amaryllis, who was sitting shuffling papers and as an outsider would be the automatic scapegoat, should one be needed.

'So - what are our aims in building this strategy?' Steve had now produced a big piece of paper, which he unrolled on the table in front of him. It was completely blank so far. 'Amaryllis, would you hand out the Post-Its, please?'

'Here you go,' said Amaryllis, handing round little clumps of the garish sticky notes. Please God, don't let him ask us to write a strategy on a Post-It, thought Christopher, surprising himself by his inner desperation.

'It's amazing what you can get on one of these,' said Steve, waving around a little bundle of bright blue ones. Christopher had deep pink, and he could see that Big Dave was embarrassed by the pale pink pile in front of him.

'I've heard tell there are monks who can write the whole Harry Potter saga on one of those,' observed Jock McLean. Steve gave him a hard look. Christopher waited for Jock to say 'Ooo, I'm really scared', but fortunately he didn't.

'I'd like you to write on one of your Post-Its what you think is the one thing this strategy will achieve,' said Steve. 'Then we'll stick them all on this big piece of paper here and that will enable us to discuss it in more detail.'

In other circumstances Christopher might have enjoyed playing around with Post-Its, sticking bits of paper together, and drawing in different colours, but not in present company. He could see Jock apparently doodling. Amaryllis had written what looked like a chapter of a novel on hers, but then she thought better of it, scrunched up the first one and threw it in her bag, and wrote just a few words on the new one.

He thought about what he would like to achieve, and the first answer that came to him was that he wanted things to move forward extremely slowly, at a snail's pace, so that the movement was imperceptible and painless to everyone. He hastily wrote 'research and consultation' on the Post-It - when it came to delaying things, these were definitely top of the list. Consulting everybody in the town would take months, if not years - even working out how to consult would take some time. Christopher brightened up a little. He smiled at Amaryllis, whom he hadn't spoken to since mentioning the kids. It was a pity he hadn't got the chance to tell her the full story, but if his delaying tactics worked, they would have all the time in the world to talk about these things.

'Chris, you look pretty pleased with yourself,' said Steve suddenly. 'Here, you can be the first to put your Post-It on the page.'

Do I get a gold star as well? Christopher wanted to ask. And don't call me Chris!

He placed his Post-It randomly on the big clean white flip-chart page. One by one Steve invited the others to do the same. Jock had produced a doodle that was indecipherable at first glance. Young Dave had only reluctantly taken time off from his lawyer's practice. 'Time is money, guys' he had said, but had given in on a vague promise that he would get some new legal business out of it, although come to think of it, he would probably be disqualified from using his position here to his own profit.

He had written 'go down the pub' in large bold letters. Mrs Stevenson had written 'I don't know what to say' on hers, neatly summing up in one short sentence almost all her previous contributions to all discussions she had taken part in. The boy who had come along with Steve and introduced himself as a youth worker but who looked like a layabout had written 'community integration' on his. Christopher suspected Steve would pounce on this and use it to drive the debate forward.

'Research and consultation!' exclaimed Steve. 'Very good - that's just the sort of thing we need.'

Christopher searched his expression for any trace of irony, but it was completely absent. Scary that someone with this big an intellectual vacuum in his head should be helping to shape the future direction of West Fife Council. Scary, but Christopher was not all that surprised.

'Hmm,' was Steve's reaction to 'community integration'. 'Can you expand on that a bit, Darren?'

'Like, we don't feel like part of it,' said Darren the 'youth worker', doing various random basketball moves - without a basketball, fortunately for the management at the Holiday Inn, who might have had to replace all the interior fittings - as he spoke. 'There's nowhere to go. Nothing to do.'

'Ha! That's what they always say!' scoffed Jock. 'Nothing to do so we'll go and vandalise this bus shelter. Nothing to do so we'll go and beat up some poor old soul on her own doorstep...'

'Isn't that a bit derogatory, Jock?' said Steve, gentle reproach oozing out of his vocal cords like the last of the tomato ketchup out of one of these old-fashioned glass bottles. Christopher, to his surprise, had found the new squeezy ones worked much better.

'Derogatory? Ha!' snuffled Jock, absent-mindedly cleaning his pipe out into Darren's backpack. 'Turn your back for a second, you'll be toast!'

'Is that what your cartoon depicts, Jock?' said Steve.

Jock peered at his own drawing as if he'd never seen it before.

'No, don't be daft - it's an abstract work on the subject of local government.'

They all peered at the little drawing. It looked a bit like an unravelled piece of knitting.

'Moving on,' said Steve after a short respectful pause. He homed in on Mrs Stevenson's Post-It.

'Interesting,' he said. 'So in a way you feel as excluded by the whole process as Darren here does.'

Mrs Stevenson and Darren gazed at each other with mutual loathing. Christopher guessed that each was finding it as difficult as the other to be lumped together in this way.

'So - what have we got left?' said Steve. Was it just Christopher's imagination, or was his tone sounding increasingly desperate? He reached Young Dave's effort and smiled in a strained way. 'Yes, here we have another one who feels dissociated from the process. How about you, Dave?'

Amazingly, his face relaxed at last as he read Big Dave's Post-It. 'Listen, you guys, we can work with this.... Point one: survey potential users. Point two: get quotes for building work. Point three: ask for the money. We really can work with this....What can I say? Let's start with point one.'

'You've forgotten mine,' said Amaryllis coldly.

She indicated her Post-It, which lurked at the side of the big piece of paper, hovering on the threshold as she had

36

done herself the previous week, awaiting acceptance into the group.

'Research and consultation,' said Steve blankly. 'But we've already had that one. And it comes into Dave's as well.'

'Because it's the most important,' said Amaryllis. 'Because if nobody wants to do any community activities, we might as well not bother.'

'Not necessarily,' said Steve. 'As a Council we have a duty to provide leisure facilities for the local community we serve, whether they want them or not. We would be negligent if we didn't. Someone could sue us. No, we may stir up a previously unsuspected demand if we get this project up and running. Sometimes the egg has to come before the chicken.'

'If you build it, they will come,' said Mrs Stevenson. 'It worked for Kevin Costner.'

Christopher opened his mouth to start explaining to Mrs Stevenson the difference between real life and the movies, then closed it again without speaking at all. There were certain conversations you just didn't want to start.

'Well, since you're both so interested in this aspect of the strategy, why don't you form a sub-committee to look into research methods,' said Steve smoothly. Christopher could hardly believe his own tactic was being used against him like this. It didn't help that when he caught Amaryllis's eye she was looking at him as coolly and calmly as the fishmonger or butcher might look at the pathetic thing on the slab that had once been a living creature. About to dissect him, was she? We'll see about that, he thought.

'Great idea, Steve,' he heard himself saying with false bonhomie.

'And why don't you, Darren, work together with Jock and me on the master plan?' Steve continued in similar vein. Jock's mouth, open to receive the cold pipe he would suck like a baby's dummy in moments of boredom or stress, stayed open in startlement. For his part Darren laughed derisively, then shrugged his shoulders.

'My social worker never said it would be fun,' he said in a kind of low growl. He reviewed this statement and corrected himself almost at once. 'Well, yeah, she did say it might be fun. Lying cow. Main thing is, though, I have to come along as part of the conditions of supervision. Doesn't matter to me what I do when I get here.'

'Mrs Stevenson and the two Daves? I'd like you to form a social sub-committee. Keep us motivated with coffee and cakes, eh?'

'Coffee and cakes?' said Young Dave incredulously. 'And by the way, Dave and I don't like it when people do that.'

'Do what?' Steve sounded genuinely curious. As far as anything he did could ever be genuine.

'Lump us together,' said Big Dave. Suddenly he was back to his usual self, looming over Steve with the look of someone who could tear him apart with his bare hands, before breakfast. 'We don't like it at all.'

Steve held up his hands in apology. 'Consider me warned off. It won't happen again.'

'And we don't like coffee and cakes,' said Young Dave. 'In fact, why not all go for a beer right now? This place sucks.'

'Well, it's against Council policy to mix alcohol and meetings,' said Steve.

'The writ of Council policy only runs as far as we let it,' said Young Dave mysteriously.

'I think you'll find that's - ' Steve began.

'And don't start telling me what's legal and what isn't,' said Young Dave, 'because I can out-jargon you any day. Right, then, last one in the Queen of Scots gets the drinks in!'

'Oh, Dave, you naughty boy!' said Mrs Stevenson. 'You know I can't run as fast as you with my hip.'

'We're not going to the Queen of Scots,' said Steve.

'See you at the bar!' shouted Amaryllis, scooping up her long black leather coat and understated leather shoulder-bag, and sprinting out of the room like a teenager.

'Wow, she's fit!' said Darren, gazing after her. 'In all senses of the word. Where's this Queen of Scots place then?'

'Just follow us,' said Big Dave as he and Young Dave left the room. Darren collected his backpack, sniffing suspiciously at its interior, and went after them.

Mrs Stevenson lumbered to her feet.

'Come on, last one there's a jessie,' she said to Jock McLean. The two of them limped out of the room, almost in step but not quite.

Christopher and Steve Paxman were left looking at each other. Steve stroked his beard in huffy silence. Christopher had only stayed out of a misplaced sense of responsibility. He was picturing Amaryllis running lithely along the road outside, looking like Atalanta before she was distracted by the golden apples.

'They'll come back when they're ready,' said Steve, gathering all his papers together, neatly folding the large piece of paper with the silly Post-Its stuck on to it and shoving everything in his school satchel-style briefcase.

'But we haven't got a lot of time - have we?' said Christopher.

Steve shook his head.

'The grant application has to be in before the end of the year. Even then it'll be touch and go. I'm sure you realise, Chris - '

'Christopher'.

' - yes, sorry, that you may not get funding for this new venture of yours. That we might have to look for alternatives.'

Christopher didn't like the implication that the whole village hall project had been his idea, but then he wasn't sure how they had all got into this situation in the first place. One minute Steve had been looking into PLIF for no apparent reason, expecting it to have a lot of paperwork in place, and wondering why they hadn't restored the hall already, and the next minute they were meant to invent a community strategy for the town off the tops of their heads. He couldn't work out how they had been so easily swept out of their comfort zone and into the main current of Council policy. It wasn't as if the Council had shown any interest in them previously. As far as he could recall, PLIF had been born out of boredom one wet spring evening in the Queen of Scots. He couldn't even remember exactly whose idea it had been. It seemed to spring simultaneously into the minds of several people, and had taken shape over the months without the benefit of any aims, objectives or constitution.

'So we have to go through all this strategy and sub-committee stuff to be in with a chance, but even then we might not get anything,' said Christopher, summing up the situation for his own benefit. He drummed his fingers on the table. 'Even jumping through all the hoops might not be enough.'

'You need to have a strategy document in place and a tactical plan for carrying it out,' said Steve, reverting, as most dictators do when it looks as if the battle isn't going their way, to quasi-military terminology. By now Steve had put on his black leather jacket and was on his way out the door. 'Could you just close the windows for me? I need to be in Auchterderran - ' he checked his watch in a token gesture, ' - about half an hour ago.'

Scowling to himself, Christopher obediently closed the windows, scooped up his own old black leather jacket and put it on, wishing he didn't now feel as if he was just copying Steve Paxman. There was somebody he didn't want as a rôle model. He'd be trying to grow a silly-looking beard next.

Chapter 4 You say gorilla and I say guerilla

'So it's war,' said Christopher a few days later in the Queen of Scots. 'Only we don't have any generals, or big guns, or any equipment for that matter.'

He had mulled over the situation after leaving the Holiday Inn. PLIF – his group of friends – their cosy evenings in the Queen of Scots - Steve Paxman's vaguely threatening manner and proposal to involve the local council in something they had no right to get involved in – and he had decided to make a stand. It wasn't like him to dig his heels in, but he felt responsible for the whole thing, and wanted to do what was best for Pitkirtly. In any case, he knew this was the one area of his life where he had any chance of exerting any control; his rôle in the community anchored him, in effect, to the kind of reality he wanted to live in. If he lost that, he would be adrift in an open boat.

'A guerilla campaign,' said Amaryllis, who had listened intently. This close attention in itself unnerved Christopher, since Amaryllis's intentness seemed to him more aggressive than many other people's active hostility. 'We'll have to fight a guerilla campaign. That's what local activists do when they have no power and very few resources.'

'Yes, I think some of us know that already,' said Jock, who before he retired had attempted to teach history to a bunch of ungrateful teenagers who were only interested in themselves. Christopher had often heard him ranting on in this vein, sometimes for hours on end.

'Gorillas? Those big black hairy things they keep in the zoo?' said the alleged youth worker Darren, perfectly illustrating the point Jock had made on numerous occasions about education being wasted on the young.

Jock gave him a quick rundown on the history and logistics of guerilla warfare, while the rest of them talked among themselves about the allotment situation, among other pressing local issues. Mrs Stevenson was particularly vocal on the topic of organic gardeners and their general pickiness and intolerance. They had given up trying to explain it all to her. Amaryllis showed a polite interest and enquired about getting an allotment, but was quickly left with the impression that it was impossible unless your parents had been particularly far-sighted and had put your name down for it well before your birth.

Once Christopher called the meeting to order, after a fashion, they talked a bit more about the guerilla campaign.

'You're not just using the term in a loose populist sense, meaning a guerilla marketing campaign, are you?' said Young Dave. 'Only I'm not that keen on marketing myself.'

'Nobody's asking you to market yourself!' said Big Dave scathingly. 'You wouldn't get many takers, that's for sure!'

'It's got nothing to do with marketing,' said Amaryllis. 'Well - only in the sense that we need to sell people on our own ideas before the Council come along and present their ideas wrapped up with red tape.'

'What are our own ideas then?' said Jock McLean, ever the stirrer.

'We don't need to bother about that yet,' said Amaryllis airily. 'They can't be worse than the ones the faceless apparatchiks at the Council come up with.'

Christopher noticed how she relished the phrase - it lent a gleeful air to the whole sentence, like a lovely sunrise spreading light and warmth across the earth. He paused for a moment, rewound his thoughts and wondered when

43

he had started to think like a revivalist preacher. He just hoped the tendency hadn't come out in his speech too, without him noticing.

Amaryllis had discarded a couple of layers of clothing as she became more and more relaxed in the company of PLIF. She was leaning forward slightly to emphasise what she was saying. The sight of her chest in a tight-fitting top seemed almost too much for some of their number. Jock McLean was leaning forward too, and Big Dave, standing over them all as he often did, apparently to emphasise further how much bigger he was than any of them, had bent so far towards her that he almost fell over. Steadying himself he noticed Christopher looking at him, and said gruffly,

'The lassie's quite right. Faceless apparatchiks.'

'All we need is to know what outcome we want, and everything else follows,' continued Amaryllis. She sat up straighter and glanced round at the group members. 'So - what do we want?'

'We want things to stay as they are,' said Young Dave wistfully. He was young enough to think that particular outcome was possible or desirable.

'Don't be daft, man!' said Big Dave. 'Things don't stay the same. Either you embrace change or it washes over you like a massive wave full of the rubbish that people flush into the sea these days.'

'Have you ever written a poem, Dave?' said Amaryllis.

Big Dave blushed.

'Well, it's funny you should say that, but I once won a prize for poetry.'

'Sometimes you sound very poetic. Maybe if we do get the village hall off the ground we should try and start a writers' group. Anybody else interested?'

There was a silence. In fact Christopher himself dabbled in writing from time to time, and on one occasion when he had had to escort Mrs Stevenson home because she was too drunk to stand up properly, she had shown him a whole suitcase full of her writings. Apparently she had written twenty-three novels, all unpublished. He hadn't had the heart to ask her why she bothered. Presumably the activity must fulfil something inside her. Christopher found it unsettling even to think about all this, but he wasn't sure why. Perhaps it was the sad waste of potential, perhaps that nobody would ever see the novels....He had resisted the temptation to offer any help with getting them published, since he realised that by the following day she would have forgotten she ever showed him the suitcase.

'We want to improve the town,' said Christopher, remembering vaguely that had been their reason for nurturing the infant PLIF in the first place.

'In what way?' said Amaryllis. Honestly, the woman was worse than Steve Paxman. Or even Jeremy Paxman.

He shrugged his shoulders. 'Make it a better place to live.'

'Better than what?' Amaryllis persisted. 'Better than Torryburn? Better than Burntisland? Better than it used to be in the eighteenth century?'

'What did you retire from?' said Christopher, finally losing patience with her. 'The KGB?'

She was silent for just a moment, then rallied with, 'You wouldn't believe me if I told you.'

He wondered if he had imagined the fleeting expression of panic in her eyes. Surely Amaryllis wasn't an underground Al Qaida operative?

'I think we're losing track of the agenda here,' she added. 'You want to improve the town - how? By building a new shopping mall, or encouraging people to keep their houses in better condition, or putting up new street lights, or painting the school pink? Or none of the above. Tick as applicable.'

'None of the above,' said Jock McLean. 'There are plenty of shops already. As long as I can still get my pipe tobacco and a haggis from time to time. What we need is another pub where other people can go so we'll have more room in here. It's getting a bit crowded these days.'

He stared pointedly at a noisy group of women who were exchanging hugs and squealing like teenage girls.

'I'm guessing the Council won't cough up for a new pub,' said Young Dave. 'They're more likely to go for painting the school pink, in my experience. Or running clubs for lesbian single mothers.'

They were seeing a whole new side of Young Dave, thought Christopher, and probably not his best side either. He had a lot more irrational prejudices than Big Dave had, and there was a whining undertone to a lot of his speeches that really wasn't very appealing. Christopher didn't like stereotypes, but what did anyone expect from a lawyer?

'Look out,' said Jock McLean in an undertone. 'Bandits at three o'clock.'

'Bandits?' Christopher's bafflement caused him to glance all round, and, fatally, to catch someone's eye.

The swarm of squealing woman had formed itself into a phalanx with a bright-haired, well-groomed woman at its head, and was coming straight for them in a menacing fashion. Taking eye contact as encouragement, the bright-haired woman accelerated.

'Got to go,' muttered Young Dave, slithering expertly from his chair and sliding past the swarm without meeting anyone's eye.

The lead woman, or queen bee as Christopher couldn't help thinking of her, stopped at their table and addressed them. There was a low buzz in the background from the rest of the group, about seven in number. Since the others were all female too, Christopher assumed they were worker bees.

'Is this the Local Improvement Forum meeting?' she asked, smiling. Her teeth were white and perfect, which identified her as American, had her accent not already done so.

'Not really,' said Christopher. He didn't feel the need to say any more at this stage. Unfortunately she did.

'We've heard tell that you're the big shots around here. That if we want anything done we should approach you... Well, we want something done.'

She stared at him as if daring him to ask what she wanted done.

'I think you've been misinformed,' said Christopher, as politely as he could manage considering that it was nearly the end of a long and trying evening. 'Even if this was a meeting, we don't have any power or official remit.'

'So you won't help us?' she said, staring at him without blinking in a way which reminded him unpleasantly of a lizard. She had a face of a rather reptilian shape, now he came to think of it.

'Tell us what you want,' said Amaryllis, perhaps sensing deadlock. 'And we'll see if we can be of any help. This is Christopher, and my name's Amaryllis.'

'Well, now, that's very neighbourly of you,' said the queen bee – or leader of the lizard pack, if that was the collective name for a group of lizards – and pulled up a chair to sit down at their table. The rest of the swarm, now humming amiably enough, gathered behind her. She gave Christopher a sour look, smiled at Amaryllis and said,

'My name's Maisie Sue McPherson? From Idaho? We've started a quilting group, right here in Pitkirtly!'

There was a pause, then Amaryllis said smoothly, 'That's – interesting.'

Christopher admired the way she said it – almost as if she meant it.

'The Quilting and Embroidery League of Pitkirtly?' said Maisie Sue. 'QELP. We're affiliated to the International League of Quilters. We plan to compete in the Quilting Olympics.'

'Oh, really?' said Amaryllis, now sounding faint with amazement - or possibly suppressed humour, Christopher thought. 'I didn't know quilting was an Olympic sport.'

'To be truthful, it wasn't one of the original Olympic sports,' said Maisie Sue, 'but what else would you call an international competition to find the best in the world? Anyway – don't let me run on, dear, I get carried away once I start – we were just setting around my kitchen table one afternoon eating blueberry muffins, when the door opened and what do you think?'

'I can't imagine,' said Amaryllis.

Jock McLean had started to edge away, no doubt hoping to melt into the crowd at the bar before anybody noticed, but Christopher gave him a look and he moved back towards the table again. Christopher had a momentary qualm of guilt, which he then immediately

48

rationalized by asking himself why Jock shouldn't suffer with the rest of them.

'The Easter bunny came in with a basket of chocolate eggs?' he suggested to Maisie Sue.

'But it was only the twenty-third of February!' said Maisie Sue reproachfully. 'No – Mrs Fotheringham came in and there wasn't anywhere for her to sit!'

She paused; Christopher, Amaryllis, Jock, Big Dave, Darren and Mrs Stevenson looked at each other. Christopher tried to work out from the others' expressions what this last sentence had meant, but they all looked as baffled as he felt.

'There wasn't anywhere for her to sit,' Maisie Sue repeated, no doubt used to Brits being slow on the uptake. 'That was when I knew.'

'You knew?' said Christopher and Big Dave, almost but not quite in sync.

'I knew we had to find somewhere else to meet!' said Maisie Sue. There was a louder, more agitated buzz from the swarm. It definitely sounded threatening. Maisie Sue fixed big blue eyes on Christopher. 'I know you can get us a place to hold our meetings.'

'What makes you think we can do anything about it?' said Christopher, conscious of Amaryllis at his side – he imagined she would be smiling and nodding, but he couldn't tear his gaze away from Maisie Sue's for long enough to find out. He guessed that the rest of the group would lose any interest now that Maisie Sue had turned out to want something from them.

Maisie Sue shook her head. Her blonde curly hair didn't move – Christopher decided it must be glued to her skull. The swarm started to look ugly again.

'I just don't understand you Brits!' said Maisie Sue in a low dangerous voice. 'How can you sit there and say that? If you had any get-up-and-go you'd have built yourselves a village hall by now instead of sitting there drinking your English pints and talking about things!'

'I'm afraid if we had any get-up-and-go we just wouldn't be British,' said Amaryllis. Maisie Sue stared at her, and then the perfect teeth showed themselves again in a grin. She started to laugh. Christopher didn't see the joke but he smiled anyway.

'As it happens,' he said, unbending a little, 'we're about to consider a project to refurbish the old village hall. Maybe you'd like to join in with the fund-raising.'

By 'join in' he of course meant 'run'. He imagined Americans – especially the slightly scary, domineering kind like Maisie Sue – would be rather good at that kind of thing.

'Great!' said Maisie Sue. 'Just say the word, and we'll do anything we can – leaflets, banners, bake sales, lobbying... When can we start?'

Christopher had the all-too-familiar sense that events were about to run away with him. He opened his mouth to try and fob the women off, but Amaryllis came to his rescue again.

'Let me take your mobile number and email address,' she said firmly to Maisie Sue. She keyed the information into her phone and produced a business card from her pocket which she handed over.

'I thought you said your name was Amaryllis,' said Maisie Sue suspiciously. 'This card says you're Yelena von Strohheim. That sounds kinda foreign to me.'

'Whoops,' said Amaryllis. She took away the card and, after a bit of rummaging, found another one to give to

Maisie Sue, who scrutinised it carefully. 'It's all right,' added Amaryllis. 'The other one wasn't mine – somebody gave it to me at a Star Trek convention.'

'That is so quirky and wonderful!' said Maisie Sue. Fortunately Amaryllis's quirkiness seemed to have satisfied her for the moment. She got up and led the swarm out. Christopher felt as if all his energies had been drained and he would need to lie down for a while to recuperate.

'Interesting,' said Amaryllis, eyes narrowed. 'I wonder what that approach meant.'

'What?' said Jock, surprised out of his self-imposed silence. 'It was about the Quilting Olympics, wasn't it?'

Mrs Stevenson laughed scornfully. 'Of all the silly ideas – that ice-dancing stuff was bad enough.'

'I like ice-dancing,' said Big Dave. 'Not doing it, mind – just watching.'

'Americans never do anything for just one reason,' said Amaryllis. 'There must be an ulterior motive behind it.'

Christopher wondered what sort of experience she had based that conclusion on.

The meeting broke up shortly after that - it was fairly obvious to Christopher at least that they had run out of sensible conversation. Amaryllis insisted there should be at least one action point, and by a narrow majority they had voted for her to think of an action that would really annoy Steve Paxman. Of course all the others could have thought of several annoying things before breakfast, but the woman was so keen, it was a shame not to take advantage of it.

Christopher had to leave promptly, because he had something to do that evening. He caught Amaryllis's eye but didn't make the mistake of mentioning kids again.

Maybe after a while she would forget about them. Although it might have been better to tell her the full story from the start.

This just wasn't the right time.

Chapter 5 One of our council officials is missing.

Once again Christopher found himself making his way through the narrow cobbled streets near the Queen of Scots, and on up the main road with Amaryllis. The others had all gone in different directions. It was getting towards dusk, and there was a spring drizzle in the air, and the smell of fallen cherry-blossom that had been trodden into the pavement. He tried to say something that didn't mention the kids, and failed miserably.

'I've got to get back and help Faisal with his history.'

'So - how many kids have you got? And other appropriate questions,' said Amaryllis.

'I wasn't even going to mention the kids,' said Christopher, blushing. 'Are you doing anything nice this evening?'

'Not really, unless you count curling up by a log fire with a book and a large glass of Australian wine,' she said. 'And a box of Belgian chocolates within reach in case I feel like a nibble.'

He smiled.

'That sounds good. What kind of book? Let me guess - a thriller.'

She gave an unexpected start then shrugged her shoulders and replied, 'No, anything but that actually. Chick lit, history, satire.... No, I don't usually enjoy thrillers. Too much blood.'

That surprised Christopher: she seemed like exactly the kind of cool, detached, analytical person who would like the puzzle element of thrillers. And the danger, surely. It was slightly odd but there you go. They said goodbye at the school gates and went their separate ways. Christopher for his part went straight home, following a well-trodden route past the bowling-green and down the long avenue with the beech trees on either side.

Amaryllis's route was more circuitous.

Dodging behind a parked car in a street just round the corner from the school, she ran along the pavement bent almost double, shielded from view by two of the four wheel drive monsters the street was notorious for, then stood upright again to saunter down a lane leading into the next street, politely greeting an old man walking his fox terrier. Running lithely in the manner that had made Christopher think of Atalanta earlier in their acquaintance, she made her way down towards the shore: she could have been a jogger, or just someone in a hurry to catch a bus, or to get home in time to see 'Strictly Come Dancing', except that halfway down the road, after a quick glance round, she left the pavement, climbed over a garden wall and then made her way through a series of gardens. She was mostly unobserved but was shouted at once by a protective mother whose toddler strayed into her path. Emerging at the other end of the terrace, she took off her jacket, turned it inside-out and put it back on again, took a scarf out of her bag and tied it round her head, then sauntered back along the front of the houses, in no hurry at all.

Amaryllis was, in private life at least, quite an incurious person who didn't tend to wonder about other people's lives. She had spent too much time on her own to be interested. But as she sauntered round the corner and back up away from the shore again, she found herself picturing Christopher, this evening clad staidly in a green parka with a fake fur-trimmed hood worn over a tweedy sports jacket, making his way steadily home to his family. She wondered vaguely why he had discarded the worn leather jacket that had made him look so much like a teacher or youth worker.

Her information was that he lived in an unconventional setup, but she hadn't bothered to memorise all the details. How old were the children? Had he mentioned teenagers? Was he married or not? Did he, his sister and the problematic children share a house with a wife who looked like a female version of Christopher himself? Did she have wispy hair and a round shiny face; did she wear tweed a lot? Did she resent the sister's presence and nag at him constantly to get rid of his troublesome sibling? No wonder he chose to be so involved in PLIF and spend so much time at the Queen of Scots!

Amaryllis almost regretted not doing more research into this setup – but she would only have been doing it out of idle curiosity in any case. It was really nothing to do with her. Christopher and his life were on the periphery of her sphere of interest. It was only because she was going soft and had let herself get out of practice that she was even thinking about them.

Damn! She had been walking in the same direction for too long. Amaryllis glanced round to check out who else was on the street. Two old people hobbling along away from her - no, it was just Big Dave and Mrs Stevenson, probably sharing their physical woes or debating the finer points of the allotment hierarchy. A teenage boy on a bicycle endangered himself and others by stunt-riding to and fro across the road just behind her. Was he following her? If so, it was probably just out of aimless malevolence towards people of her age, and not for any more sinister reason. It wouldn't do any harm, though, to disappear now just in case.

Amaryllis turned sharply on her heel and ran across the road and in through the side gate of the nearest house.

The boy on the bicycle spoke into a mobile phone. But she was already gone, over the back fence of the house and into the scrubby little park that was the only place in town for people to exercise themselves, their children and their dogs. It was a constant battleground among these different user groups. In a better world, thought Amaryllis, jogging along the main path with the air of someone who did this every evening in all weathers, there would be more parks, and walks, and dedicated play areas where kids were safe. And nobody would be cruel to fluffy bunnies, and nobody would ever try and blow anyone else up for any reason, real or imaginary. This world was far from ideal.

The fair-haired man in grey walked towards her.

Amaryllis's pace slowed as they got closer to each other.

'You're not meant to make contact with me,' she hissed crossly. 'I've retired.'

'It's an emergency,' he hissed in a passable imitation of her tone.

'We need more cover,' she said. 'Wait five minutes and then come round the back of the Sports Centre.'

'Ooh, sounds a bit dodgy,' he mocked. 'Will we be smoking round there – or doing something more interesting?'

She didn't dignify these suggestions with an answer, but speeded up again, continuing to run along the main path through the park. Seven minutes later, they made their rendezvous behind the Sports Centre, by the dustbins. There was a lingering smell of cigarette smoke in the air. The Sports Centre didn't entirely live up to its name, having been converted from an old cricket pavilion and with space only to offer a few lockers and the choice of table tennis or snooker. Amaryllis had noticed there were usually more young people hanging around at the back than she had ever observed entering the building. Fortunately the smoking area was deserted today. She diagnosed football on television as a probable cause.

'Nice ambience,' he commented, leaning on the wall by the back door. Why did he always appear so nonchalant, so unruffled by events around him, even when he had engineered them himself and their explosiveness had got out of hand? She remembered that she had never liked him.

'OK, Simon, what have you done with Steve Paxman? And why? He wasn't part of the deal.'

'I know that now! I can't help it if he's a dead ringer for the woman's brother.'

'He isn't a dead ringer. As you would know if you'd been paying attention. He was just wearing a similar jacket, and it was getting dark… You weren't meant to snatch the target on his own anyway. It's the woman that needs protecting. And the kids.'

Amaryllis paced up and down. She opened one of the bins and glanced inside. She replaced the lid, frowning.

'That was just Phase One,' he said with dignity.

'Where is he, anyway?'

'In a safe place.'

'This could put everything in danger. Everyone.'

'I'll sort it. I just need you to do one tiny thing.'

'Ha!'

'Just try and calm him down. The brother, I mean – he keeps staring at me as if he's suspicious. I don't like it.

57

It's going to make him jumpy when the time comes. Tell him I'm from HMRC or something.'

She snorted with laughter. 'That's supposed to set his mind at rest, is it?'

'He doesn't have anything to hide, so it won't bother him. He has all the hallmarks of a pathetically honest law-abiding citizen.'

'All right, I'll try,' she said, preparing to resume her jog through the park by re-tying the lace on one of her trainers, and pretending to do a few stretches. She didn't entirely trust Simon Fairfax. But that was all part of the game she thought she had left behind.

Amaryllis knew she would be on a high by the time she got home, unable to relax or sleep, still expecting the phone call that brought bad news, or the electronic call to action. She really should try and finish the process of training herself to live like a normal person, but after years of high-powered activity it was proving to be extremely difficult.

As she let herself in through the front door of the first floor flat that overlooked the river and carried out the sequence of checks that would show whether an intruder had been in there while she was out, triple-locked the door behind her and drew the curtains before opening the windows, Amaryllis thought again about Christopher and his cosy little life. She didn't know whether to feel envious or disdainful. Was it possible to feel both at once? She prowled around the flat, twitching once or twice at the curtains to watch the moonlight turn the tops of the waves silver against the blackness of the night river.

Christopher opened his own front door with a certain amount of trepidation. He never knew what sort of mood Caroline might be in. Or Marina, for that matter. There were a lot of raging hormones around the place these days, and he was very wary of them. At least Faisal was straightforward and easy to understand. He didn't ask much either, poor boy, just a bit of help with his homework now and then. Faisal had been quick to appreciate that Christopher was more use with things like history and English and up to a point French, than with maths, although at random times Christopher found his school arithmetic came flooding back to wash over him, along with unwanted memories of other aspects of his school career. He had spent most of his teenage years hiding from various people, school bullies both pupils and staff, and his parents. And his sister, of course.

No shouting tonight. So far, so good.

It was slightly too quiet if anything. Sinister, almost. For a moment he had the ignoble thought that maybe they had all gone, and his spirits lightened fractionally. Then Caroline came down the stairs.

'Hi,' she said. 'Faisal's stuck with his history again. How can they expect them to know about the Stuart succession? He knows more about Iranian history than he does about Scotland.'

Don't say 'and whose fault is that?' Christopher told himself sternly. He couldn't think of anything else to say.

'There's something for you in the freezer, I think,' said Caroline off-handedly, and carried on into the sitting-room, where, he noticed, the television was on. Marina must have started the evening's viewing early tonight. He suppressed a pang of longing for the times when he had been able to call his house his own, when he could have had a quiet meal in the kitchen with a book, or carried his plate through to the sitting-room and put Shostakovich on the cd player. And he could have had a glass of wine without worrying that it would start Caroline off again.

He hung up his jacket and went to look in the freezer. Hmm. OK, he was a carnivore whereas the others were all vegetarians, but Bird's Eye frozen roast beef in gravy? Honestly, he did have certain standards. He looked in the fridge for an egg, and ate it scrambled on toast, while sitting at the kitchen table and reading the local free newspaper.

'You haven't eaten the last egg, have you?' said Caroline, coming into the room and looming over him. 'Marina needs it for breakfast.'

'I'll go and get some more,' he said.

'You'd better hurry, the Co-op closes in ten minutes.'

'Oh, God.' He got up from the table, wondering why kids weren't trusted to run errands like this nowadays. He had a distinct recollection of being sent out to the local shop for bread at quite a young age - seven or eight, perhaps. Maybe Caroline had similar memories.

On the way back from the Co-op - they hadn't had any free range eggs so he had had to buy battery ones, which he disapproved of, battery chickens reminding him of school children and office workers in so many ways - he looked down the road towards the shore. It was tempting to go on down there and just to keep on walking, away from his home and the life that had grown so restrictive - but towards what? Freedom? He was inclined not to believe in the concept. Was it the empty space that was left when everything else had gone? Or was it something more positive than that - something that gave you an adrenalin surge and made you want to leap and shout?

He put the eggs in the fridge and sat back down with his newspaper and a cup of tea. Caroline came into the kitchen.

'Have you helped Faisal with his homework?'

'I will in a minute,' he said.

It was worse than being married! There must be some dynamic about a man and woman living in such close proximity that made them nag and squabble and score points off each other.

He stared at the front page of the paper. It was the local West Fife daily. He had bought it for the jobs page: not that he really expected to find anything suitable in it, but he had a compulsion to keep looking. Christopher knew well that anyone advertising for an archivist would probably use 'The Scotsman' or the media section of 'The Guardian' or perhaps these days an online facility; in any case the chances of a part-time archives job cropping up in Pitkirtly were miniscule, yet he couldn't go full-time or move away while the kids still needed him.

He was putting off the inevitable moment when he would turn to the jobs page and find nothing there again, when a photograph on the front page caught his eye. Surely that was –

He read the headline next to the photo and a shiver went down his spine.

'West Fife community worker missing,' proclaimed the larger headline and, underneath in smaller print, 'Police appeal for information.'

He read on down the column.

'Community worker Steven Paxman, 43, has been missing from his home in Aberdour and from his office in Auchterderran for several days after failing to turn up at a meeting with colleagues on Tuesday.

'Police are puzzled by Mr Paxman's disappearance and concerned for his safety. They have appealed for witnesses who may have seen him at any time on Tuesday. He was not known to have any family or work problems, was in good health and apparently in good spirits when he last contacted colleagues by phone on Tuesday afternoon.'

Christopher pushed the paper aside. He had to ring the police; he was somewhat surprised they hadn't already been round, but perhaps Steve Paxman hadn't told his colleagues his plans for Tuesday evening so nobody knew he had been meeting the people from PLIF. He pictured Steve putting on his jacket and picking up his briefcase at the end of their meeting. Where had he gone? What could possibly have happened to him after leaving that sterile conference room?

Caroline came into the room again.

'What about Faisal's homework?'

'I'll do it now.'

Christopher wondered what Caroline would say if she knew what a shock he had just had. Probably nothing, unless she could find a way in which it related to her. He decided not to tell her anything about it. She would only mock him later when Steve Paxman turned up large as life, having in the mean-time won the lottery and gone on a luxury cruise, or having fallen down the stairs on the way out of the Holiday Inn and been sent, no doubt, to a private clinic for treatment to make sure he didn't take legal action against the hotel company.

He would be better to get Faisal's homework out of the way before calling the police.

By the time he and Faisal had wrestled with the Stuart succession it was past ten. Coming downstairs, Christopher wondered if it was too late to ring the police.

They would probably think it was an emergency, and it wasn't. The right people might not even be on duty. He had just decided it could wait until the next day when the front door-bell rang.

Caroline emerged from the living-room, glass in hand, grumbling away either to Christopher or to herself.

'It's OK, I'll get it,' said Christopher quickly.

This was enough to encourage Caroline to lurch towards the front door and fling it open.

Accelerating down the stairs, Christopher raised his eyes and saw two policemen standing on the doorstep. Before Caroline could speak, he called,

'Are you here about Steve Paxman?'

He reached the door at last, sliding past Caroline as he did so.

'Mr Wilson? May we come in, sir?' said the older of the police officers, displaying identification. Sensing that there was only one possible answer, Christopher stood aside and made what he hoped they would interpret as a welcoming gesture.

'Come in,' he said, to make it absolutely clear. 'We can sit in the kitchen.'

'Do you need me for anything?' said Caroline, surging into the path of the younger policeman as he entered the hall. Christopher willed her just to go away quietly; he tried not to let that show in his face, but concentrated on leading the way to the kitchen.

'I don't think so, Mrs Wilson,' said the older policeman, giving her a passing glance. 'We'll let you know if we do.'

'It's Mrs Hussein,' said Caroline, and headed for the living-room again, perhaps recalling that she had left a bottle there.

Christopher sat at one side of the kitchen table with the two police officers at the other. The older one nodded to the younger one, who took out his notebook and pencil. He seemed nervous; his eyes darted from side to side, and he frequently shifted in his chair, twisting his body as if he wanted to see if there was something creeping up behind him. The older one did most of the talking.

'You are Mr Christopher Wilson? Chair of an organization known as Pitkirtly Local Improvement Forum?'

Christopher nodded. 'Is this to do with Steve Paxman?'

'We're trying to establish the current whereabouts of Mr Paxman, yes, sir. One of his colleagues mentioned that he might have been meeting you on Tuesday evening.'

'Yes, we had a community strategy meeting at the Holiday Inn,' Christopher admitted, trying not to let his scepticism about the exercise seep into the words. He didn't want them to think he had been in any way hostile to Steve Paxman although in many ways he had indeed felt like that.

'Community strategy, eh?' said the older police officer with a sceptical grin. Christopher was wary of a trap, so he remained silent and poker-faced. A few seconds later he began to worry that his failure to return the policeman's grin would be seen as a sign that he had something to hide. But it was too late to change his reaction by then.

'So Mr Paxman was at the meeting, was he? What sort of time would that be?'

'Yes – from about six-thirty to eight-ish, I suppose,' said Christopher, trying to remember when the great escape to the Queen of Scots had begun.

'And you all left together?'

'Yes – well, no. The others left, then I had a few more words with Mr Paxman, then we both left. No, he left the room first and I closed the windows and then went too.'

'You don't seem all that sure. It's only a couple of days ago.'

'I'm sure now I've thought about it. The others were in a hurry to get to the pub, and I thought I'd better have a word with Mr Paxman about what had happened at the meeting – what would happen next, that kind of thing – and I stayed on a couple of minutes longer to speak to him. He asked me to close the windows because he was running late. I think he said he was expected in Auchterderran.'

'And then?'

'Then? – I closed the windows and left. I went to the pub – the Queen of Scots. That's where we go.'

'And you didn't see Mr Paxman again on your way.'

'No,' said Christopher, mentally replaying the walk from the Holiday Inn to the Queen of Scots. It would have been a pleasant walk if the veiled threats of Steve Paxman hadn't still been hanging around him like a swarm of midges, small but intensely irritating. An avenue of trees led from the Holiday Inn, which was situated in a converted minor stately home known locally as the Castle, to the main road. Come to think of it, it was quite surprising that he hadn't at least glimpsed Steve Paxman at some point – but the man probably had a fast car or even a souped-up motorbike.

'You didn't see his motorbike then?' said the younger police officer suddenly.

'Motorbike? I don't think so.'

Christopher replayed the walk in his mind for the second time. He had wandered off the hotel drive and into the trees to avoid being mowed down by Range Rovers or whatever was the current car of choice for the kind of people who stayed at the hotel, and he had a vague memory of a black car passing him at a fair speed on the way down to the main road. He started to open his mouth to mention it, then he realised he would seem silly if he had no idea what make of car it was, never mind not having memorised the number-plate in case it turned out to be relevant. He realised that, despite having a good eye for detail in his working life, he would make a useless witness in court.

'No. No motorbike,' he said at last. 'Do you think he had an accident somewhere?'

'Not on his motorbike, sir,' said the older policeman. 'He left that in the car park at the Holiday Inn.'

'Strange,' mused Christopher.

'What about the others?' said the older police officer.

'Others?'

'The other members of your group. Are they all well-known to you? Local people?'

Christopher's thoughts flew to Amaryllis. He couldn't claim to know her well, exactly – and yet. And yet in another sense he felt as if he had always known her, which was such an odd feeling that it rendered him temporarily speechless.

'Mr Wilson? Can we have the names and addresses of those present on Tuesday?'

He complied as far as he could, only now realising he didn't really know the people he thought of as friends. Out of all of them, he could only provide addresses for Jock McLean and Mrs Stevenson.

'I'm afraid that's all,' he said. 'But of course, only a handful of people are keen enough on doing things for the community to take part in PLIF at all. People can be amazingly apathetic.'

'We understand that,' said the older policeman. He nodded to the younger one, who snapped his notebook shut so loudly that it made Christopher think, in an unfortunate mental leap, of a guillotine. They warned him he would have to make a formal statement at the police station the following day.

'Don't leave the country,' one of them joked as they left. From the hall they could all hear Caroline enthusiastically joining in with a late edition of Top of the Pops.

'Good voice,' one of them commented.

Christopher closed the door behind them with relief, and leaned on it for a few moments. Don't leave the country? If only he could!

He contemplated the nature of freedom again later that night as he lay in bed trying to block out the noise of the television from the room below. He was even tempted to abandon the house - his own house - to Caroline and her offspring and go and live elsewhere. It might almost be worth it....but every time part of his mind strayed down that primrose path, a more rational part reminded him of how much he had always liked the house, with its sunny situation and view of the river from the top windows, and the garden he and his father had worked in together. It didn't mean as much to Caroline: why should she have it?

A prisoner in his home and even in his thoughts, Christopher at last fell asleep.

Chapter 6 Signals from another world

At the suggestion of Amaryllis, and because Christopher wanted to avoid another onslaught from the Quilting and Embroidery League, the PLIF steering group took the revolutionary step of arranging to meet in a different pub, the Elgin Arms down by the harbour. It was older and more picturesque than the Queen of Scots, but Christopher didn't like it as much. The doors opened directly on to a main road, for one thing, whereas the Queen of Scots was tucked away in a jumble of old crooked houses, which gave the illusion that nobody could find it if they didn't know it was there. In fact he knew the Queen of Scots had been mentioned in several tourist guides to this area of Fife, and in the high season would probably be over-run with pretentious legal personnel from Edinburgh, which was another good reason for checking out the alternatives.

'It's too twee,' said Jock McLean, furiously sucking on an empty pipe. He glared at the curtains, which Christopher didn't think most people would consider twee, since they had rather a masculine dark stripe on a kind of tweedy fabric, but which presumably offended Jock merely by being there.

'The beer's no use,' said Big Dave.

'It's full of incomers and tourists,' said Young Dave, who had been an incomer himself only a couple of years before. In his own legend he was now more local than the locals.

'Has anybody else seen the police?' said Amaryllis, pale green eyes sparkling. Christopher thought the change of scenery suited her. 'About Steve Paxman. Does everybody know?'

Mrs Stevenson struggled into the bar.

'It's too near the water here,' she said. 'Doesn't do my arthritis any good, you know. My knee's killing me after walking down that slope.'

This was quite a long speech by Mrs Stevenson, but like Amaryllis, she seemed to be exhilarated, in her own quiet way, by sitting in a different bar, though still with the same woolly hat and the same Dubonnet to drink, obviously.

'Here,' she said, taking off her coat and putting it carefully on the back of her chair. 'I've had the police round.'

'About Steve Paxman?' said Amaryllis.

'What else would bring them to my door?' said Mrs Stevenson. Her pique at even being asked the question vied with her need to share what had happened, and the impulse to gossip triumphed. 'They're saying he disappeared right after that daft meeting we had the other night up at the Castle.'

'Castle?' said Amaryllis. 'Oh, you mean the Holiday Inn!'

'It's always been the Castle to me,' said Mrs Stevenson. 'You used to get proper gentlemen staying up there, not those girls who wear glitter and nothing else.'

Jock McLean and Big Dave suddenly started to pay attention.

'Maybe we should do a reconstruction up there with some of those girls,' suggested Jock with an evil smile. 'See if we can jog anybody's memory. Or anything else.'

'I think we just need to co-operate with the police, that's all,' said Christopher.

'They asked me what time you got to the Queen of Scots,' said Mrs Stevenson, looking at him accusingly.

69

'I was the last to leave the room at the Holiday Inn,' Christopher admitted. 'Steve Paxman got me to close the windows. He was in a bit of a hurry.'

'So you might have been the last person to see him alive!' said Mrs Stevenson.

'I don't think there's any reason to think he isn't still alive,' said Christopher, framing his sentence carefully. 'He could have lost his memory – or fled the country – or have been called to a relative's bedside without having time to let anybody know. The policemen didn't say what they thought had happened.'

'But they're concerned for his safety, though,' said Big Dave. 'It said so in the papers.'

Amaryllis broke her silence to add, 'He would have got in touch by now if he could.'

'There you are!' said Mrs Stevenson.

'But what could have happened to him in Pitkirtly?' said Christopher, not really wanting an answer. 'It's not as if it's the murder capital of the world or anything.'

'That's Detroit, isn't it?' said Big Dave.

'Cape Town, mate,' said Young Dave.

'I expect he'll turn up again wondering what all the fuss is about,' said Mrs Stevenson comfortably, taking a sip of the Dubonnet Big Dave had already got in for her.

Amaryllis, by contrast, still seemed to be on edge, fidgeting with one of the zips on her leather jacket and intermittently glancing round at the rest of the bar population.

'So is this a normal meeting of PLIF, or what?' said Young Dave.

'There's no such thing!' crowed Jock McLean, cheering up slightly. 'This is as normal as it gets.'

'So what's on the agenda then?' Young Dave challenged Christopher.

'Item 1, apologies. I take it Steve Paxman won't be able to make it,' said Christopher, becoming infected by the general mood of frivolity. 'Item 2, the guerilla campaign. Item 3, the village hall.'

There was a groan round the table.

'I was asked if the village hall could be put on the agenda,' Christopher explained.

'Who by?' demanded Young Dave.

'Who do you think?' returned Big Dave.

'Yes, I asked for it to be added,' said Amaryllis. 'We should at least talk about it - if nothing else, it'll give you the chance to air your reasons for being so against it.'

Christopher knew, and Amaryllis had probably worked it out by now too, that they wouldn't be persuaded to air their real reason, which was that they didn't want anything to change. There would be all sorts of feeble justifications - the state of disrepair of the building being one of the more serious ones.

'I'll air a reason right now,' said Young Dave. 'If it does belong to the town, then the townspeople would be better served by knocking it down and selling the land for building. You could get a nice new block of apartments, right near the river, double-glazing, balconies - it'd be a gold-mine.'

'You're not in court now,' said Jock McLean. He knocked his pipe out on the edge of the rather nice tile-topped table. The barman looked over suspiciously in their direction. Jock stuffed his pipe into his jacket pocket.

'You can't just rob me of my chance to speak by making sarcastic comments,' said Young Dave.

'Oh, can't I?' said Jock McLean. 'Have you got any more to say?'

'Um - no.'

'Well, let somebody else have a go, then, lad.'

Christopher opened his mouth to speak just as Jock said smoothly, 'What do you think, Mrs Stevenson?'

'If the Cooncil want to pay to have it re-built just so young hoodlums can wreck it again, that's their own lookout,' said Mrs Stevenson, face nearly as pink as her drink.

'We haven't really got to that agenda item yet,' said Christopher, getting his word in quickly before Jock and the Daves started again.

'There's no need to talk about the gorilla campaign any more,' said Big Dave. 'Been there, done that. It's redundant now himself's gone.'

'Well, what else is on the agenda?' demanded Jock.

'Item 4,' said Christopher reluctantly and very quietly. 'The PLIF Midsummer party.'

The reason he was reluctant was because of what had happened at the PLIF Christmas party, or, more accurately, because he couldn't remember what had happened there, although rumour, started by Big Dave, had it that Christopher had taken all his clothes off and insisted on going for a midnight swim in the River Forth, during which activity he had had to be rescued from almost certain death by a couple of off-duty policemen wielding a life-belt and one of these long poles that lifeguards in swimming-pools sometimes have. He was sure he would have remembered that. The shock of the ice-cold water would have sobered him up, for a start.

'And?' said Jock.

'Item 5. AOCB. Item 6. Date and venue of next meeting. That's it.'

'Taking that last point first,' said Amaryllis, 'does Steve Paxman have to come to the next meeting? Assuming he's still – with us, so to speak.'

'Oi!' said Big Dave. 'It's only the chairman that's allowed to take the last point first.'

'And sometimes not even the chairman,' added Christopher. It was obviously time to assert his authority. How he hated those occasions. 'OK,' he said while he still had the floor. 'Dave's right, there isn't really much more to be said about item 2 at this stage. We already have an action point in hand for it, and progress is being made.' He refused to ask Amaryllis if she was indeed making progress with her action point of doing something to annoy Steve Paxman. The man had already taken up more than enough time at the meeting, without even being there. Christopher knew if he didn't stay focused he would lose control of the meeting again. 'Item 3. The village hall. Steve Paxman seems – seemed - to want us to go for it. Does anyone have any views?'

He knew everyone had views, the question was whether they were prepared to come out with them or not.

'What I want to know is,' said Young Dave,' why we need both items 2 and 3 on the agenda. Surely they're mutually exclusive.'

''I don't understand what you mean,' said Amaryllis.

'Well, mutually exclusive means - ' began Young Dave self-importantly.

'No, I mean I don't see why they are mutually exclusive in the first place,' Amaryllis interrupted him.

Christopher knew that if there was one thing guaranteed to end in tears, it was Young Dave trying to explain in words of one syllable something that everyone else in the room understood better than him. Mrs

Stevenson had walked out of a PLIF meeting in protest a few months before when he had insisted on deconstructing the word 'deconstructing' in exhaustive detail. Big Dave had had to be forcibly restrained soon after that when Young Dave told those remaining what a hypotenuse was, using a makeshift diagram drawn in spilt beer on the table-top.

'Well,' said Young Dave, reasonably happy now that he had more or less been begged to explain something, 'if we're against the Council, and the Council are in favour of the village hall being restored, why do we have to have a guerilla campaign? No, that's wrong - if we're in favour of the village hall and so are the Council - no, what I mean is, why are we against the Council if they're offering to spend money on the town?'

'We're not necessarily against them,' said Amaryllis, 'but we don't trust them to do it right without monitoring what they do and preparing to fight against it if we have to.'

'So we're not about to fight them just yet?' said Young Dave, cheering up a bit. Christopher suspected that at least some of his legal work originated with the Council's various departments, or tentacles as cynical people might call them, and he didn't want to kill the goose that laid the golden egg without having a few ducks and maybe some chickens hidden away in a hen-house up the road.

'We just want them to be aware that somebody's keeping an eye on them,' Amaryllis confirmed. 'What about the village hall project, then? Anybody in favour?'

'Will they have tea-dances?' said Mrs Stevenson.

'Not unless somebody wants to organise them,' said Amaryllis.

'Good,' said Mrs Stevenson. 'They're the work of the devil.'

Everyone waited in vain for her to elaborate on this bald statement, but she just took another sip of Dubonnet and looked enigmatic.

'You all know what I think,' said Young Dave.

'How about you, Jock?' enquired Amaryllis. 'Do you think the town needs a focus - somewhere for people to go?'

'A focus?' said Jock, leaning back so far in his chair that it looked as if he might fall over - Christopher remembered this as a skill many teachers had. 'We've already got the church and the war memorial,' Jock continued.

It was impossible to tell whether this was one of his jokes. It wasn't funny, but it might have been a very subtle attempt at humour. Jock wasn't himself a church-goer, allegedly believing time spent in church to be time stolen from his allotment, but he did have a great respect for tradition.

'What about non-believers?' said Amaryllis.

'They're all welcome in church. They're all God's children,' said Jock piously, and then suddenly roared with laughter. 'I got you all going, didn't I?'

They all laughed dutifully.

'Aye',' he continued, 'anything that draws people away from the grip of the church can't be a bad thing. This village hall's got my vote.'

'I'm not so sure,' said Big Dave, frowning in concentration. 'Is it not just a waste of money like Young Dave was saying?'

'What would they spend the money on otherwise, though?' Jock pointed out. 'They'd just pour it down the drain. It wouldn't come to Pitkirtly, that's for sure. It would go into Low Eglinton and Higher Hillfield to help people who should be helping themselves. Picking up the pieces after a whole lot of drug addicts and alkies with kids they have no idea how to look after...'

Christopher hoped Amaryllis didn't object to all this political incorrectness. He wasn't sure, although as far as he could tell from her expression, she found it very laudable. Her hands twitched as though they wanted to applaud at the end of Jock's speech.

Then the door to the bar opened, bringing a flurry of showery rain, a fairly brisk wind and a fair-haired man in grey. Christopher thought Amaryllis was disturbed by this new arrival: she didn't jump, in fact the opposite if anything - she sat even more still than before, the faint smile wiped instantly from her face and her shoulders tensed. She didn't look in the man's direction, but she didn't deliberately look the other way either. The man in grey went to the bar and ordered a drink, then stood there with it, surveying the scene. His gaze didn't linger on Amaryllis, but he must have registered her presence along with the others.

'Look,' whispered Mrs Stevenson, nudging Christopher, 'that young man over there. Do you think he's a spy?'

'A what?'

'A spy. A secret agent. A spook. He's got a look of James Bond about him. Not Sean Connery. The other one.'

Once again Mrs Stevenson had blurred the lines between fantasy and reality until nobody knew where to start arguing with her. In any case, there was no denying that the man had a sinister look about him. He just didn't fit in. His suit was too good, or at least it didn't look as if it had been bought off the peg in the PDSA shop, and his hair was too modern for Pitkirtly.

'So,' said Amaryllis in a lower voice than before, 'how about you, Christopher? Do you have an opinion?'

'Well, if there were a middle way - ' began Christopher.

'What, a middle way between restoring the hall and knocking it down?' said Jock scathingly. 'Wouldn't that be just leaving it as it is?'

'I thought that was what everybody wanted,' said Christopher in self-defence.

'But is that what you really want?' breathed Mrs Stevenson, leaning towards him in a way that made him think of the Wyrd Sisters. He wondered if any of her ancestors had been suspected of witchcraft.

'It doesn't matter what I want,' said Christopher. 'It's whatever's good for the community.'

He had unintentionally spoken more loudly than before. Amaryllis glanced at him with a worried look and said, 'Sssh, we don't want everybody to hear what we're talking about.'

It didn't seem to have bothered her before, even when Big Dave was booming away, so perhaps the man in grey was responsible. Christopher lowered his voice. 'If in our judgement the community would benefit from having the village hall restored, then we should support the project whole-heartedly - whether the Council does anything about it or not.'

He thought about it for another moment as they watched, and added, 'I think we're divided enough on this to take a vote.'

'Do we have a quorum?' said Young Dave, obviously afraid of being defeated.

'Chair plus two makes a quorum,' said Christopher, consulting the PLIF constitution which he had been foresighted enough to bring with him. 'All in favour?'

As expected, Young Dave was the only one who voted against the restoration of the village hall, and equally predictably, he went into a sulk.

Amaryllis went to the Ladies soon after that - and didn't come back.

The man in grey also left the bar shortly after that.

For his part, Christopher had an uneasy feeling that this wasn't coincidental and that the fair man in grey was following Amaryllis. He muttered something to the others, grabbed his parka and made his way out to the street as quickly as possible. Once on the pavement he glanced from side to side - and saw that the fair man was doing the same thing, about twenty metres along the street beside a very shiny black car. Christopher stepped back into the pub doorway, but he had an uneasy feeling that he had been spotted. And where had Amaryllis got to? Even if she had gone out the window of the Ladies' - assuming it had a window and one that was big enough for someone to wriggle through, and that it didn't lead to a completely enclosed yard she couldn't escape from - as far as he knew all the exits from the pub faced out on to this road, the one that ran alongside the water. The pub was built into the side of a cliff, and there was a persistent rumour that if you ventured behind the bar you would find an old smugglers' tunnel that led into the hillside and emerged -

Christopher had a sudden idea. It wasn't exactly a flash of inspiration but more of a slow burn, with an uneven light that only illuminated parts of the puzzle. He put on his parka, which he hadn't had time to do before, turned up the collar against the cold wind, and set off along the street, in the opposite direction from where he was really heading. He tried to walk in as normal a way as possible, but had to fight against the tingling between his shoulder-blades and the sense of being followed. He didn't look round. But he paused at the information board which displayed a grim story from the past, when there had been a watch tower in Pitkirtly, and a siege from the sea, and various people had met horrible grisly deaths. He had never read it properly before, since his interest was in genuine historical records and not in a 'heritage' worker's interpretation of them in the light of what people today were likely to be interested in. He didn't read it properly now, just peered at it in a pretence of interest, as if he were a tourist or visitor to the town.

He looked up.

The fair man in grey was sauntering towards him.

He tried not to panic. After all, how likely was it that any harm could come to him here, in his home town, as small, insignificant and sleepy as any other in West Fife? He was only a hundred metres or so from the cosiness of the pub where his friends were still drinking. On the other hand, he was also ten metres from the deep icy darkness of the water in the harbour, and there might not be any off-duty policemen around this time to fish him out with a pole.

Two more things happened in quick succession. A police-car came slowly down the hill and drew up in front of the Elgin Arms, and the fair man turned tail and hurried back to the sleek black car, which then started moving, gathering speed as it passed Christopher. For a moment he pictured what it might have been like if the car had been accelerating straight at him as if the driver were trying to knock him over the harbour wall, and then he blotted that out of his mind.

He hesitated, wondering whether to go after Amaryllis anyway and make sure she was all right, but then Big Dave emerged from the pub with one of the policemen, and waved to him, so he told himself firmly that Amaryllis could look after herself better than he could, and he walked back over to join his friends.

'Funny thing,' said Mrs Stevenson, 'that policeman said somebody reported a disturbance.'

'There wasn't one, was there?' said Christopher, deciding on the spot never to come into the Elgin Arms again. This kind of odd unsettling incident never happened in the Queen of Scots.

'No,' said Young Dave. 'Where's Amaryllis?'

'I don't know,' said Christopher, although he was fairly sure he did know, to the nearest half-mile or so, at least. 'I think she's gone for now, though. Will we consider the meeting closed?'

'No way!' whined Young Dave. 'We still have a few agenda points to get through. And we don't need Amaryllis. She isn't really a member of PLIF. Nobody's elected her. She just turned up and muscled in. She could be anybody - a Council spy - an escaped psycho -'

'All right,' sighed Christopher, although he knew there would be hell to pay when he got home, the meeting having gone on longer than expected with this interruption. 'Item 4. The PLIF Midsummer party.'

'I put this on the agenda,' said Jock proudly. 'You can't start planning these events too soon.'

'We don't usually start planning it at all,' said Big Dave. 'The last time we just turned up at the Queen of Scots one week in December and ended up having a party.'

80

'I think it could benefit from some planning this time,' said Christopher. 'Otherwise it's only an excuse to get even more plastered than usual.'

'And what's wrong with that?' asked Big Dave. 'Isn't that what those pagan festivals are all about?'

'Not exactly,' said Christopher cautiously, afraid of being shouted down by Jock in one of his rants against all, some or no religions. 'Maybe we should think about something a bit different.'

'If it ain't broke, don't fix it,' said Young Dave darkly.

'Who says it ain't broke?' Jock challenged him.

'As long as it doesn't have to be a tea dance, I don't mind,' said Mrs Stevenson.

'Well, what are the options?' said Christopher. 'Not a tea dance - I think we can all tentatively agree on that one - and not just an orgy of drunkenness and misbehaviour.'

'Not so fast, man,' said Big Dave. 'We haven't exactly ruled that out yet.'

Christopher's patience was fast running out. If nothing else was happening in the world it was all very well - and often very amusing - to sit in the Queen of Scots listening to the argument go round and round in circles before meeting itself coming back, but he had been seriously disturbed by the man in grey, and he was vaguely worried about Amaryllis, although he kept reiterating to himself that she was well able to look after herself, and he was worried that Caroline would have started drinking before he got home, and altogether he just wanted to get out of the Elgin Arms and get on with his life.

'Well then, should we arrange to go out for a meal?' he asked; then, clutching at straws, 'Or go into Edinburgh to see a show? We can't do the pantomime in the middle of the summer, but maybe we could save that for Christmas.'

As soon as the word was out of his mouth, he regretted it, knowing he had unintentionally started something that could run and run, and which just as you thought it had run its course would start up again like a clockwork toy with faulty clockwork.

'Sorry, is that the time?' he improvised, standing up again, 'I've got to go. I said I'd play Scrabble with the kids. Can we take the rest of the agenda as read, and fix the date of the next meeting for two weeks tonight? Sorry.'

As he scurried from the room he caught Jock McLean saying, 'I've never seen the point of it myself. Men dressed up as women - girls in tights slapping their thighs - '

'Mm, sounds cool to me,' said Young Dave. 'Hey, maybe we should - '

And the door of the Elgin Arms slammed behind Christopher, and he stood irresolute on the pavement outside again.

The pantomime argument always followed the same route, but with a slightly different script and, curiously, with different people playing the parts. The last time it had cropped up, Young Dave had taken the Jock McLean panto-sceptic role, while Big Dave had stepped into the part of hyper-male person consumed with lust, which, Christopher had to admit, Young Dave played much more convincingly.

Mulling all this over, he found his steps had taken him up the hill a bit and into Merchantman Wynd. He was startled; although he had been thinking about the street earlier in the evening, he had had no conscious intention of setting foot in it. Surely Amaryllis would be long gone by

82

now, even if she had indeed following an ancient secret smugglers' passage from the Elgin Arms into the hillside behind and come up through a trapdoor in the floor of the old village hall as he had surmised. The more he thought about it, the sillier this surmise became. She must have wriggled through the window in the Ladies' and been out of sight before anyone else realised she had gone.

He turned in his tracks, deciding firmly he would go on home and face whatever was happening there. He wasn't cut out for this kind of thing. He didn't spell out to himself what kind of thing he was thinking of, mainly because he didn't want to frighten the wits out of himself.

As he paused before going on his way, he heard a noise.

It wasn't the scream of a lady in distress, or even a shout or a gunshot, all of which possibilities had run through his mind at some point during the evening, just a kind of dull thudding sound in the middle distance. Manfully ignoring all the shadows and dark shapes lurking round the apartments of Merchantman Wynd - which seemed to have been designed to encourage the wildest of fantasies - he made his way towards what seemed to be the source of the sound. Surprise, surprise, he was heading straight for the village hall.

The dull thudding sound paused for a moment and then resumed. As he turned his steps into the yard, he could hear a faint voice too, though he couldn't distinguish any particular words. Was somebody shouting for help?

He pushed at the door to the hall tentatively, in case somebody was standing behind it. There were more shadows and shapes in here, patches of deeper darkness in the darkness. A small amount of light filtered in through the holes in the roof, from streetlights outside the building, giving the place a sinister orange-yellow glow.

The thudding came from a corner in what must have once been a kitchen. They had only glanced into it the other day, not interested in details until they knew the bigger picture.

Christopher approached the sink, taking small steps in case the floor wasn't safe.

'Help me!' called the voice, and the thudding resumed. It was coming from under the sink. Christopher wanted to run screaming from the place; only the idea that it was Amaryllis who needed his help, and the guilty feeling that he should have done something to help her earlier, kept him here.

He opened the door to the cupboard under the sink. It fell off its hinges at once, causing a huge amount of noise.

'Who's that?' said the voice, quite close now.

'It's Christopher. Christopher Wilson.'

'Thank goodness for that! Get me out of here!'

'But how - ?'

He peered at the interior of the cupboard. The wall behind it had been reinforced with a panel that looked almost new, with massive shiny screws all round it to secure it in place. His heart sank.

'Can you wait until I get help? Or I could go home for my Phillips screwdriver with the interchangeable heads?'

'No!' she yelped - he had identified her as Amaryllis by now.

'But there's a new panel in here - I won't be able to shift it by myself.'

'Get something to break it down with,' she called. 'Those new kitchen components are made of cardboard.

You should be able to do it with one hand tied behind your back.'

Christopher didn't stop to debate this with her, although in fact he was completely useless when it came to breaking things down, putting things together or anything to do with home maintenance and improvement. Caroline had gone so far as to suggest he take a course in it. As if she would notice if the house fell down around her ears.... He poked about in the corner of the room, trying to find something - anything - that would lend strength to his arm as he attempted the impossible - all the time hoping somebody better qualified than he was would come along at the vital moment.

'Hurry up!' was the faint cry from under the sink. 'I need to get out of here - really, really need to, I mean!'

There was such an urgency in her voice that he pulled himself together, picked up a piece of old piping - probably made of lead, to judge by the vintage of the hall itself - and attacked the panel with it. After a couple of blows whereby he injured himself, jarring his elbow, without making any impact on the panel, he noticed that a faint indentation in the centre was now starting to get a bit bigger, with one or two cracks appearing around it. He focussed the next couple of blows on that spot, and a hole appeared.

'Nearly there,' he muttered over-optimistically. It took a bit longer, and took reserves of strength he hadn't realised he possessed, to break right through and release Amaryllis.

'Thank goodness for that,' she wheezed as she climbed through the gap. 'There were some seriously nasty spiders in there.'

'Spiders? You had me getting repetitive stress injury in my elbow just because you don't like spiders?'

'It isn't a case of not liking them,' said Amaryllis, moving away quite speedily. 'It's a phobia. If I get particularly scared I start to wheeze and then the next step is anaphylactic shock. But I should be ok,' she added airily. 'Now I'm in the open air.'

'How did you get in there in the first place?' said Christopher, fishing for extra information. She turned and gave him a look.

'So you don't know already? You just happened to be walking down Merchantman Wynd when you heard the noise I was making, and came to have a look?'

'Sort of,' said Christopher.

'Liar!' said Amaryllis, proceeding out into the yard ahead of him. 'You've got it all worked out, haven't you, Mr I'm-just-a-boring-archivist- who's-led-a-very-sheltered-life? The tunnel behind the bar, the smugglers, the village hall.... it's all clear to you isn't it? My secrets aren't safe at all.'

'Secrets?'

'Metaphorically speaking,' said Amaryllis. She sounded almost as if she had been drinking, or taking drugs. But she had only nursed a half of lager in the Elgin Arms and hadn't seemed to be at all the worse for wear then.

They walked along Merchantman Wynd, together and yet separately.

'Aren't you going to ask me anything about tonight?' said Amaryllis.

'What do you think I should ask?' he countered. Although of course he had wondered about Amaryllis, the fair man in grey, the tunnel and the newly constructed wall panel under the sink in the old village hall, he hadn't considered it polite to ask. If she wanted to talk about it, then she would.

And it seemed that she did - up to a point.

'I knew about the tunnel in advance, of course,' she said. 'The Elgin Arms had quite a reputation at one time for being a smugglers' pub. It was always being raided by the revenue men. Still is, for that matter. Did you see that man in grey tonight?'

'Revenue men?'

'HM Revenue and Customs. They're checking all along the coast for smugglers. I don't think they know about the tunnel, but they might do.'

'So he was a customs officer?' Christopher said incredulously. 'I thought - no, never mind that. Why were you running away from him then, if he was a harmless bureaucrat.'

'No bureaucrat is completely harmless,' said Amaryllis.

'Yes, but why - ?' persisted Christopher.

'I knew him once,' said Amaryllis, reluctantly. 'I don't particularly want to meet him again.'

'So it was better to disappear up a tunnel where the roof may well be ready to cave in any minute, on the off-chance of some idiot passing by to get you out at the other end?' Christopher's voice rose in a fury. He couldn't quite analyse why he was so cross, but perhaps it had something to do with the fact that the man in grey, far from being the Mafioso or agent of a foreign power conjured up by his imagination, was just a civil servant who happened to work in Her Majesty's Revenue and Customs. Surely there must have been people in that organisation who were aware of the existence of the tunnel. If nothing else it would be in the HMRC archives, if such a repository existed.

'I could have gone back down to the pub if I had to,' she said softly. 'I thought I would exhaust all other possibilities before I embarrassed myself and surprised some innocent woman by popping up in the Ladies again unexpectedly.'

They came out of Merchantman Wynd and walked on up the hill, side by side but more separate than ever.

'So,' said Amaryllis, looking at him sideways. 'What about those kids of yours?'

'What do you mean, what about the kids?' parried Christopher.

'Well, are they real, for a start?' asked Amaryllis outrageously. 'There's no evidence of them apart from hearsay - I've asked around and neither of the Daves has ever met them or has any idea how old they are or anything. Maybe you just made them up to cover for something else.'

'Oh, they're real, all right,' he said. 'But I don't feel like discussing them with you at the moment.'

'Well, that's me told,' said Amaryllis. 'This is where our paths diverge, Christopher. I'll see you around.'

She bounded off round the corner, laughing. He stared after her, all sorts of different emotions struggling with each other for top spot. But in the end he had to squash them all down inside him again and trudge off home to see what was waiting for him there. It wouldn't do to bring his own emotions into the situation there - there were more than enough to go round already.

Chapter 7 Harmless bureaucrats

The man from HM Revenue and Customs was waiting at the corner of Christopher's road the following morning, a Saturday, but as Christopher approached he jumped in the black shiny car and drove off. Coincidence, thought Christopher - or was it? He wasn't going to become paranoid about this. The man must have far bigger fish to fry than Christopher. Whether Amaryllis was a big fish or not was open to question - the only way to find out, presumably, was to reel her in. Since he had no idea how to do this, Christopher decided he wasn't interested in the answer.

He walked on down the hill towards the harbour. The route was a lot less scary in daylight - no dark shapes lurking in even darker shadows, no mysterious thuds down dark side streets. No imagined pursuit by faceless bureaucrats. No sightings of Amaryllis. He hadn't come down here expecting to see her, but for a healthy bracing walk along by the harbour, and a chance to think about things clearly without the constant background noise in the house from Caroline, the television, and Faisal's computer games.

He thought about whether he could cope with the kind of things that seemed to be happening in his life now - the changes to his former routine, the possibility of still more change, the presence of Amaryllis, Steve Paxman and the fair man in grey in his circle of acquaintances. He thought about Amaryllis, the litheness of her stride, the air she had of being ready to spring into action. She was so different from him that until he had met her he might not have thought it possible for her to exist in the same universe as him. Certainly not in the same little local organisation - for Christopher harboured no illusions about the importance of PLIF.

He thought about his older acquaintances, a few of whom had perhaps now qualified as friends, though he wasn't absolutely sure of that; it would depend on how broad your definition of friends was. Jock McLean was probably the most similar to him; then again, he would never share those schoolroom memories and manners with Jock. There was a special quality about those who were or had been teachers: some sort of fatalism, perhaps. In the case of Big Dave, they were on friendly terms but Christopher didn't think Big Dave really needed friends: he could take people or leave them, without turning a hair. Young Dave - Christopher actually paused his steps here to think - he didn't want to stigmatise Young Dave just because of his day job, but as a lawyer he probably only hung out with people he could use and not necessarily with those he liked.

'Hi!' called Young Dave just at that moment from the other side of the road. He was jogging. He waved a friendly hand as he passed. 'See you at the Queen of Scots tonight?' he added as he passed. Was that friendship? Christopher pondered - or was there something particular that Young Dave wanted? It must be very difficult for lawyers to make friends: that was quite likely why they almost always congregated with their own kind, clogging up certain wine bars in the New Town in Edinburgh, annoying people with their uniformity and the way they sucked in wealth like leeches feasting on blood. Some people would have taken the figure of speech further, but Christopher felt it was already quite unfair enough.

A shiny black car drew up a few metres further along the harbour front. Christopher was suddenly on edge again, his contemplative walk ruined. He pictured himself being kidnapped, dragged into the car in broad daylight, watched by the morning dog walkers, joggers, and people fishing along the harbour wall: it had happened before to other innocent men and women, perhaps not in this precise spot but somewhere. He could be taken away and murdered in a field at the back of beyond, his body thrown down an old mine-working or left in undergrowth for a Labrador to sniff out in the distant future, when he could only be identified by dental records and everyone had forgotten what had happened to him. 'What happened to old Christopher?' one of the Daves would say. 'One minute he was there, chairing the PLIF meeting, the next minute he was gone. Never did leave a forwarding address. Must have wanted to get away from Caroline and the kids.'

The irony was that at times when he had been at the end of his tether with Caroline he had spent quite a number of sleepless nights trying to work out a foolproof plan to disappear without trace. It was always the national insurance number that was the tricky part. You couldn't get work, or a pension, or benefits, without it. He had tried to imagine the life he would lead on the streets, begging for small change to buy fries at Macdonald's, sleeping under a bridge or at a disgusting hostel. Somehow these fantasies were always set in London, though he had no doubt there were people living like that much nearer home. It was the fact that London was so big and anonymous that made it the right place for these flights of fancy - surely it must be the best place to lose yourself in.

He didn't care for the kidnap option as a way of disappearing. He wished Young Dave had actually stopped to chat for a while instead of jogging on past. He wouldn't have minded talking to Mr Revenue and Customs about what his problem was, if Young Dave had been with him. Whoever was in the car couldn't, surely, have kidnapped both of them at the same time. And with Young Dave's grasp of legal and bureaucratic jargon they might have been able to straighten out the whole thing - whatever it was.

Christopher tried to work out what he might have done to attract the attention of Her Majesty's Revenue and Customs. What had he brought back with him from the long weekend in Brussels he had managed to snatch before Caroline had clamped down on his foreign travel? He couldn't imagine he had been over the limit for going through the green channel at Customs. Even if he had, it wouldn't have justified the presence of a shiny black car. He had the impression they were reserved for pursuing big time crooks.

He had been walking very slowly towards the car all this time, and when he drew level with it, the man in grey got out at the passenger side and blocked his way. Oh, my God, it's all coming true, thought Christopher. He sensed his feet, now apparently beyond his control, stopping in their tracks. He heard his voice, thin and croaky, saying, 'Excuse me, please'. But the fair man didn't move out of his way.

'Mr Wilson? Christopher Wilson?'

'Yes. I'm Christopher Wilson.'

'May I have a word with you, sir?' The man produced a plastic-coated id card which he flashed in front of Christopher's eyes. 'Simon Fairfax. HM Revenue and Customs.'

Don't get in the car; don't get in the car, said Christopher to himself.

'Would you like to get in the car, sir? It's a bit chilly standing out here.'

'Thanks,' said Christopher, and was about to get in when he remembered all his self-talk and added, 'But I don't think I'll get in the car. I suffer from claustrophobia, you see.'

It wasn't strictly true unless you defined claustrophobia as a phobia about getting in cars in which you were likely to be driven towards death and oblivion in an abandoned mineshaft miles from anywhere.

'That's fine, sir, I just thought you might be more comfortable sitting inside. Could we walk on the harbour wall instead?'

The harbour wall! screeched Christopher's inner wimp. Are you mad? He could easily push you off and say it was an accident - and then you'd be having lunch with the fishes for all eternity.

'OK, fine,' he said, sternly telling the inner wimp to shut up. After all, there were other people about, and he was probably over-reacting to the whole situation anyway.

They crossed the road and set off along the harbour wall. There were white horses beyond it, and even inside the shelter of the harbour the little boats were rising and falling on the waves in a way that reminded Christopher uneasily of his trip across the Bay of Biscay as a teenager. He had never really been keen on leaving the country since then.

'So,' said Simon Fairfax, striding out easily on the cobblestones. 'You're chair of a community group, aren't you?'

'PLIF, yes,' said Christopher. 'I mean – Pitkirtly Local Improvement Forum.'

'Yes. And I understand a new member has joined the group recently.'

'Yes.'

'Amaryllis Peebles?' prompted Simon after a pause during which he obviously expected Christopher to produce the name.

'Yes. She isn't strictly speaking a steering group member, but we have co-opted her to assist with a particular project.'

Christopher found it amazing how easy it was to slip back into this kind of phraseology even after a while away from the workplace. Perhaps he could set up in business himself teaching people meaningless phrases for all work situations, with an advanced module on combining the phrases into sentences.

'Do you know anything about her background?' said Simon Fairfax, turning side-on to Christopher and flaunting a classical profile.

'Background? We don't usually look into people's backgrounds. It isn't necessary on our steering group. It isn't as if there are child protection issues involved, or....'

'So you're not aware if she has - for instance - a police record?'

'What sort of police record are you talking about?'

'Well, let's just say she isn't all she seems.'

'No, let's not say that,' said Christopher, who was developing more and more of a dislike of the other man as the conversation continued. 'Let's say that if you want me to believe you, you'll have to give me chapter and verse. Evidence.'

'Of course, I should have realised that as a former archivist you'd be a stickler for evidence,' murmured

Simon. He sighed. 'Well, let's just say the evidence concerns a matter of national security.'

'Ha!' said Christopher, summoning up reserves of scepticism of which he had previously been unaware. 'That's what they always say!'

'They?' queried Simon. He and Christopher had reached the end of the harbour wall. They stood there staring down into the river. The air was clear and they could see across to the other side of the Forth, where the big chimneys of the oil refinery at Grangemouth puffed smoke and occasionally fire up into the atmosphere. Christopher wondered if anyone at that side of the river was engaged in a conversation as futile as his.

'Yes, the government and the faceless bureaucrats and the police, whenever they're too embarrassed to admit they've made huge blundering errors,' said Christopher. 'They just slap an order on it and the evidence moulders away at the back of a drawer for a hundred years until everybody's forgotten about it and doesn't realise its significance.'

'Until some nosey journalist comes along and excavates the whole story, that is,' said Simon bitterly.

'Journalists! Ha!' said Christopher. They stood for one moment in harmony and mutual understanding before returning to the fray.

'So - you're expecting me to believe that Amaryllis Peebles has an unspecified record as a - what? - a criminal? a spy? a terrorist? But you can't produce the evidence because of national security? How do I know you're not just a psychotic stalker who's been following her around?'

'Because you can contact HM Revenue and Customs to confirm my identity if you want,' said Simon.

'But how do I know you're not just some psychotic stalker who happens to be a customs officer as well?' said Christopher, who was on a roll by now, and quite enjoying this conversation.

Simon sighed again, and turned his footsteps back towards land. Maybe this was the kind of conversation you could only have out on the harbour wall, where land meets sea, a place of transit and uncertainty. Maybe once they got back on solid ground it would either become more logical or Simon would drag Christopher into the shiny black car and take him away to the disused mineshaft.

'All I wanted to say,' said Simon, 'was this: please be careful of Amaryllis Peebles - she isn't all she seems - and let me know if anything suspicious happens.'

He delved into his jacket pocket and instead of a gun, which Christopher still half-expected him to be carrying, produced a neat standardised business card with a logo purporting to be that of HMRC, giving his phone number and email address as well as a postal address, doubtless situated in one of the nondescript blocks which housed his kind of operation. He handed the card to Christopher.

'Here we are. Email usually catches me quickest. Let me know about anything - anything at all that worries you.'

At the moment Christopher was hard pressed to think of anything that could possibly worry him more than his experience of the previous evening involving the old village hall and the panel under the sink. But there was no harm in taking the business card and keeping it in his wallet just in case. His instincts told him that Amaryllis was on the side of good in the eternal war against the forces of evil, but he had learned in so many ways not to trust his instincts.

As Christopher paused to put the business card in a safe place, Simon strode off, reached the end of the harbour wall and crossed the road to his car. Christopher watched as without any further ado he got in and drove off swiftly along past the Elgin Arms and round the corner. There was no knowing whether he was aware of the existence of the smuggler's passage or the opening into the old village hall. He hadn't given very much away except his suspicions of Amaryllis, which Christopher strongly suspected him of making up on the spur of the moment for an underhand reason of his own.

Christopher no longer had the heart to carry on with his walk. He had meant to make his way further along the river front and return through the woods at the edge of the town, a circular tour - something he always felt was more satisfactory than going and coming back the same way. But now that was exactly what he did, turning left and progressing quite slowly and thoughtfully up the hill again. Passing the end of Merchantman Wynd he glanced along it, straining his ears in case of any unusual sounds, but he heard nothing but the complaints of the magpies in the big trees up on the hill behind the new apartments, the whoosh of water as people tended their cars in a Saturday ceremony, and the cacophony of Radio 3 emanating from a window nearby. He could almost believe the previous night's events hadn't happened at all, only he knew he wasn't the kind of person to get lost in his own dreams and fantasies. Sometimes he wished he could do just that.

'Good morning, Christopher?' said Maisie Sue, at his side suddenly.

He jumped; he had no idea where she had come from or how she had sneaked up on him without alerting any of his senses. Now that he came to think of it, the QELP contingent had turned out to be much quieter than he had at first expected, but because of the other events in his life they didn't loom very large anyway, being a minor irritant and not a major problem. Not bees but mere midges.

She laughed at his surprise. He wasn't an expert on hair-styles or even particularly interested in them, but he couldn't help noticing that her glossy curls seemed to be arranged in exactly the same position as they had been that last time in the Queen of Scots. Either she kept her hair under very strict control using a female technique into which men couldn't aspire to be initiated, or it was a wig. It looked as if it might feel synthetic to the touch, but this was a thought that gave him the creeps.

'... thought I'd have a look-see for myself?' she was saying with a gesture towards Merchantman Wynd.

'At the hall?' he said. 'It isn't in a very good state. I'm not sure that anything can be done with it.'

It was in an even worse state now that he had vandalised the panel in the kitchen, he didn't add. She didn't need to know about that.

'It looks like there may have been vandals around,' she agreed, nodding sympathetically. 'We'll have to get hold of all the help we can, I guess.... Have you guys thought of a barn-raising party?'

'Um – no.'

Maisie Sue led the way along the cul-de-sac towards the old hall.

'I guess you guys have no need to do any barn-raising when all your farm buildings have been standing there for centuries? – I just love that! – but what if we got everybody in this village to lend a hand one weekend and made a party of it...?'

Christopher didn't want to challenge her assumption about local farm buildings – in any case, she probably wasn't far wrong – and he didn't like to dampen her enthusiasm with a cold dash of native scepticism, but his incredulity must somehow have shown in his body language. Maisie Sue added at once,

'I don't want to tell you guys what to do. I know you have your own ways, and some of them go back hundreds of years? I was just thinking, well, we were kinda hoping to find a meeting-place for QELP real soon. And that kind of fund-raising takes an awful long time.'

She actually fluttered her eyelashes at him; unfortunately for her this emphasised not just the smallness but, in Christopher's opinion, the pebble-hardness of her brown eyes. In consequence this didn't melt his heart at all. For goodness' sake, surely the woman could have got hold of blue contact lenses to make herself more appealing. If she had gone to the trouble of wearing a wig, you'd think contact lenses would only be a small step further....

They stood and stared at the building. Christopher hoped that would be enough and she wouldn't insist on going inside. He would feel bound to go with her, and that would be a complete waste of time, since he had already seen quite a bit more of the place than he wanted, one way and another.

Unfortunately she did insist on a guided tour, which he cut as short as he could. On the way back to the main road afterwards, he wondered if he was imagining the burst of mocking laughter that came from one of the balconies above them, round about the place where he thought Amaryllis lived. He had a feeling he wasn't imagining it. He didn't look up.

99

Chapter 8 A Colossal Fuss

Two things almost made Christopher late for his afternoon shift at the supermarket. One, predictably, was a task Caroline found for him just as he was about to leave the house.

'Faisal needs his football kit for tomorrow. You'd better put it in the wash.'

Caroline sat at the kitchen table reading a magazine. At her elbow rested a cup of what she referred to as 'tea' but which Christopher knew was either a very strong herbal brew or more likely an alcoholic substance.

'I'm just going out for my afternoon shift. I'll do it later.'

'Now!' she said, hardly bothering to raise her voice, and threw the cup at him without even glancing up. Her aim was reasonable, but Christopher was just quick enough to predict where the cup would go and to get out of the way.

'If he brings it downstairs, I'll put it in when I get back.'

She sighed heavily, but didn't reply. He escaped while the going was good. Not that it was ever that good if you were on your way to a shift at a supermarket. But, Christopher told himself as he turned the corner and walked briskly down the main shopping street in Pitkirtly towards his goal, he was lucky to have a job at all, especially a local one, in these uncertain times. His wages, not far above the minimum, together with what was left of his redundancy money from his previous archives career, meant survival for him and the family. He didn't like to think about what might happen when the redundancy money ran out.

He suspected his friends and acquaintances, if they thought about him and his way of life at all, had completely the wrong idea about how well-off he was. Maybe they imagined he worked at the supermarket for fun. Ha! How wrong could they be?

He was smiling to himself when he glanced up and noticed Young Dave at the other side of the road, by the knitting shop called 'Granny Can Knit' which everyone had thought for years was about to close down until the most recent outburst of knitting started. Now that people were decorating lamp-posts with knitting and making ridiculous knitted ornaments such as knitted hamburgers, Christopher supposed the place was thriving.

At that moment Darren, the young man from the strategic meeting, appeared in the doorway carrying a large bag with the 'Granny Can Knit' logo. He paused to speak to Young Dave, and the large bag somehow changed hands while they were talking. Christopher was baffled. Had Young Dave been too embarrassed to go into the wool shop himself? But if that was the case, why had he chosen someone who seemed likely to be even more embarrassed? Why not someone like Mrs Stevenson, whose natural habitat would seem to be wool shops and similar establishments?

The two men both glanced round furtively. Young Dave suddenly caught Christopher's eye before he could look away and pretend not to have seen.

Christopher waved cheerily.

'For my mum!' called Young Dave, holding up the bag triumphantly. 'She's knitting hats for sailors.'

Almost certain he hadn't heard properly, Christopher nodded and continued on down the road, puzzling as he went. He got into the supermarket just in time to hear the manager say, '… so if Chris Wilson's late one more time –'

'What's going to happen if I'm late?' he said, shrugging on his overall. 'Will it cause the extinction of all known life forms? Will we collide with Mars? Will the supermarket fall down? And please don't call me Chris.'

The manager, who had been at school with Christopher, sighed. 'I wouldn't call you it to your face. It's a different story when you're not here. You're fair game then.'

Christopher knew that, as the only one who really understood the computerised stock-taking system, he would have to do something really bad in order to get fired. He was still searching for just the right thing. Apparently it wasn't enough to use big words to intimidate the customers, to be sarcastic to the girls on the tills and to ring in sick when Caroline had one of her binges.

He half-expected, as he trudged back up the hill later in the afternoon at the end of his shift, that Simon Fairfax would be lying in wait for him on the way home to give events another twist. But the only person he recognised around the shopping area was Maisie Sue, whom he managed to sneak past as she studied the menu outside Pitkirtly's only restaurant, which in a major advance for multi-culturalism, offered both Chinese and Indian cuisine. He thought he heard his name faintly borne on the breeze as he pushed on up the street, but he wasn't going to make the mistake of turning round and catching anybody's eye. The day had been trying enough without having to converse with Maisie Sue again as well.

The day was about to get a lot more trying.

He arrived home to hear a shouting match going on; it was suddenly one of those times when he wanted to get lost in his own dreams and fantasies. Marina and Caroline were having one of their colossal fights on the stairs. Or at least, Caroline was in the hall and Marina was on the landing, so the stairs were the no man's land where if you ventured, even to pick up the wounded, you were liable to be picked off by a sniper. Fortunately there weren't any wounded - yet.

Christopher tried to get past Caroline and into the kitchen without being noticed, but it was of course impossible. Caroline swung round on him as he crossed the hall behind her.

'So where do you think you've been? Out, I suppose,' she swept on, giving the word 'out' a strange and nasty intonation as if going out was something shameful. 'Out - away from all the problems of real life, as usual. I don't know why I bother.'

Christopher didn't even reply but slid past her after all and opened the kitchen door.

'That's right, disappear while I'm talking to you!' Caroline shrieked. It didn't make sense. Not much Caroline said these days made sense. Christopher had no idea what to do about it. He had tried talking to the doctor, but there wasn't time to explain the full horror of things, and the doctor had offered him anti-depressants, which were so irrelevant to the whole situation as to be more of an insult than a treatment, only going to show how little he had taken in of what Christopher had to say.

He sat down at the kitchen table. He took Simon Fairfax's card out of his wallet and tried to decide whether to tear it up or not.

Caroline stormed into the kitchen after him. He hoped she wouldn't start throwing things again. The last time she had done that, Mr Browning from next door had come round and threatened to report all of them to the Council, the police, the fire brigade and the Queen (more or less in that order) unless they stopped fighting and arguing. He had called them an ASBO family who belonged in a council house. Christopher had known Mr Browning for about thirty years, and had never until that moment suspected him of having such ingrained prejudices.

'What's that?' said Caroline, grabbing Simon Fairfax's card and squinting to try and see it properly through the alcoholic haze.

'It's a business card,' said Christopher.

'Is it somebody from the Council poking their nose into our business?'

'No, nothing like that.'

'Well, they can take a running jump!' Caroline exploded, ripping the card in two and throwing it in the bin. Even though Christopher hadn't wanted the card, had no intention of getting in touch with Simon Fairfax about anything, and had himself considered whether to tear it up, he was furious with Caroline for doing exactly that. He had needed a bit longer to bring himself to do it.

She started on the crockery next, banging it about in the sink and muttering to herself, and after that she turned on Christopher himself, shrieking and trying to tear his hair out. He took this fairly calmly, being used to it, and managed to get away with only a couple of scratches. Usually at this point she would slump at the kitchen table sobbing, and then go into a round of apologies which were in their own way just as unnerving as the temper tantrums.

When she had got to this stage, Christopher got up wearily from the chair and went upstairs to check on the kids. Faisal was glued to his Playstation, compulsively killing aliens. The psychiatrist had advised giving the Playstation away, but Caroline had refused to do this on the grounds that she had paid good money for it. Marina had locked her bedroom door and wasn't answering any of Christopher's questions.

The front door-bell rang.

Christopher went downstairs and opened the door. He could think of people he would have quite liked to see standing on the doorstep at this point - one of the Daves, for instance, or Mrs Stevenson, woolly hat and all - and others he had no strong opinions about either way. To find a couple of police officers there was a bit of a surprise. He wasn't sure yet if it would be a pleasant or unpleasant one. He had already been down to the police station in the past couple of days to repeat and sign his statement about Steve Paxman's disappearance. But these were two different police officers, one male and one female.

'Mr Wilson?' said the policeman in a neutral tone.

'Yes,' he said.

'Is Mrs Wilson at home?' said the policewoman.

'No. I mean - there isn't a Mrs Wilson. Well, not any more. I mean, I'm divorced.'

'Since when?'

What on earth are they getting at, thought Christopher. Is this something to do with Deirdre? Has she had an accident? But they would contact Laurence, her current husband, wouldn't they?

'What's this about?' he said. 'I've been divorced for fifteen years. Has something happened to Deirdre?'

'But you live with a woman at the moment, don't you?' said the policewoman. 'And children?'

'Yes, but - '

Not knowing what it was all about, he was at a loss to know what to say next in case he incriminated himself or put his foot in it, with the latter being by far the more likely option.

'So - is your partner at home?' said the policeman, a craquelure of impatience just starting to form on his polite facade.

'No. I don't have a partner,' said Christopher, puzzled. 'The woman who lives here is Caroline Hussein. She's - '

'May we see her, please?' said the policewoman.

'If you like,' he said. 'She's in the kitchen. The kids are upstairs.'

'If I may say so, sir,' said the policeman, 'you really don't do yourself any favours being so obstructive.'

'I'm not - ' Christopher began, then shrugged his shoulders and led them into the house. The noise from the kitchen had stopped while he was upstairs, but he wasn't sure what they would find inside.

'Caroline,' he said as he opened the door, 'there are two - oh, dear!'

There was blood everywhere. It dripped off the palm of her hand on to the very attractive birch veneer laminate floor, having already, it seemed, dripped all down her front and on to her shoes, and the table, and the worktop where the kettle stood... The scene was one of a minor massacre. Even before the door was halfway open, the policeman was using his radio to call an ambulance while the woman officer pushed past Christopher and tended to Caroline with kitchen roll and sellotape.

'Is there anything I can do?' said Christopher.

'Just go and sit in the hall,' said the policeman firmly, giving Christopher rather a hostile glance. 'Don't leave the house. Don't call anybody.'

'The kids.....?'

'We'll get an officer in to be with them. Just sit down there for now. We're dealing with it.'

The policeman continued to talk into his radio. Then they shut the kitchen door.

Sirens outside, and paramedics and stretchers. Surely the children would hear all the din, even with their iPods and Playstations and other audio equipment turned up high. But they didn't come down, luckily, as Caroline, a composition in red and white with bloodstains and white, drained face, was carried away on a stretcher. Everything seemed to take a long time, and yet paradoxically the time passed quickly. The woman police officer had gone with Caroline in the ambulance and three more police officers arrived, two women and a man.

The first policeman came out of the kitchen and spoke to Christopher, who had to ask him to repeat himself. Somehow shock had affected his hearing and other senses.

'These two officers are from the family unit. They need to speak to the children. How many are there?'

'Two - Marina and Faisal. They're upstairs. Marina won't want to come out though. And Faisal won't say anything. He never does.'

'Never mind that. We still need to speak to them. They'll need to know.'

'About Caroline?'

'Why didn't you tell us she's your sister? - sir.' The 'sir' was all too obviously an after-thought.

108

'You didn't ask me,' said Christopher indignantly. 'What made you come to the door anyway?'

'We had a report of a disturbance.'

'Was it Mr Browning from next door?'

'I'm afraid I can't answer that, sir.'

'Can I tell the kids about Caroline?'

'We'll have to have officers present.'

'That's all right,' said Christopher.

'We'll do that as soon as they get here, then,' said the policeman. Christopher thought he detected a softening in the man's attitude, for whatever reason.

There was a disturbance out in the front garden. The front door stood open but apparently there were officers out there keeping nosey neighbours at bay.

'... can give you valuable information about events leading up to this...' said Mr Browning's voice, at its highest and most querulous.

There was a more subdued muttering from one of the policemen.

Mr Browning said, 'Of course I've always known he was violent - you can tell, you know. Something in the eyes... All nicey nicey but harbouring evil thoughts underneath it all.'

More muttering from the officers of the law.

Christopher had a sudden almost irresistible urge to go out to the doorstep and punch Mr Browning on the nose; however, he knew that this would not be a good time to take that kind of action. Later, he told himself, I can do it later; revenge is a dish best served cold. Perhaps that would give him time to think about administering poetic justice to Mr Browning instead - he could phone the police, for example, with an anonymous tip-off that there was a body buried under the rose bed. Mr Browning's roses were his pride and joy, so seeing them being dug up and trampled on by a heavy-footed murder squad would indeed be purgatory for him. Christopher allowed himself to smile in anticipation.

'I'm surprised you can find anything to smile about in all this,' said the policeman.

'I can't really,' he said. 'It was just a thought.'

'Neighbours been bothering you?'

'Mr Browning's a bit of a fusspot. Doesn't like noise.'

'Ah,' said the policeman cryptically. 'There's always one.'

Two more officers arrived, and Christopher was allowed to accompany them upstairs to speak to Marina and Faisal. He could tell that their ethnicity took the police by surprise and that they were having trouble working out the family relationships. He could have told them that the kids' father was an Iranian whom Caroline had met while she was an au pair in Iran twenty years before. Christopher's understanding was that she and the children had narrowly escaped with their lives when he was imprisoned for alleged activities against the regime and that she had taken up drinking as a hobby to distract herself from the fact that her husband was in daily danger of being executed. Or at least, Caroline had used all of that to rationalise her alcohol dependency and unpredictable behavior. He had a feeling she had probably had the seeds of it inside all along – certainly when they were children she had been far more volatile than he had. On the other hand, that wouldn't have been difficult since Christopher had been placid to the point of coma during the more boring parts of his childhood.

But he didn't say any of that. As a mark of respect for the children's dual nationality and culture, he usually tried to refrain from saying anything derogatory about either their mother or about the Iranian regime, which he despised and feared. None of it was their fault.

Predictably, Marina said far too much, in a colourful explosion of words which battered at everyone and rendered them incapable of speech themselves for a while; Faisal said nothing at all, and Christopher thought the police officers might have to call in a child psychologist to try and break down his silence.

Marina insisted on being taken straight to the hospital to see her mother, while Faisal hung back, not actually refusing to go but showing such reluctance that the new woman officer said to Christopher, 'You'd better stay here with him. We'll take Marina to see her mum - you look after the boy.'

'We'll leave an officer with you,' said the policeman helpfully.

'Come on, Faisal,' said Christopher awkwardly after they'd gone. 'Let's go and get something to eat.'

They weren't allowed into the kitchen, which was still being examined by the scene of crime team or whatever it was called, but one of the officers outside the front door offered to go and get sandwiches for them, not even turning a hair at Christopher's request that Faisal shouldn't have anything with either cheese or mayonnaise in it.

'I've got kids of my own,' he said comfortably. 'One of them won't eat anything except cheese and the other won't eat anything with cheese in it. Kids! Get away with anything!'

After a shaky start as far as the police were concerned, Christopher felt he was on more solid ground now. Like many law-abiding people he had felt the foundations of his world tremble when he imagined he might be on the wrong side of the law for the first time.

He and Faisal went into the sitting-room. The television was still on as a reminder of Caroline. Christopher switched it off. He wasn't sure where he stood with Faisal.

'Can we play chess while we're waiting for the sandwiches?' said Faisal. Christopher was taken aback. This was the nearest thing to a complete original sentence that he could recall Faisal speaking since the family had arrived in his house in the first place.

He took the chess board down from a shelf, blew the dust off it and started to set out the pieces. By the time the sandwiches arrived, Faisal had already checkmated him once and was well on the way to doing it again. The policeman who had gone down to the supermarket said approvingly, 'Good idea, sir. Keep his mind off things.'

The phone rang in the hall. A murmur of voices, then the first policeman put his head round the door.

'There's a Mr McLean on the phone for you, sir. Want to take it now or will I tell him to call back later?'

No end to the talents of the police, thought Christopher. Providing catering facilities, and now acting as his secretary. He looked from the chess board to Faisal's face, and made up his mind.

'I'm just about to get checkmated again. I'll call him back when that's finished.'

'It's not over until the fat lady sings,' said Faisal, surprising Christopher for the second time in fifteen minutes.

After the third checkmate and the sandwiches, he judged that Faisal was ok enough to be left in the sitting-room with the first policeman while he went and rang Jock McLean back.

'What's going on over there?' said Jock. 'It sounded as if there were people turning the place upside down.'

'That's it, more or less,' said Christopher. 'It's the police. Caroline's been taken to hospital. It's - too difficult to explain just now.'

'Drunk as a skunk, was she?' said Jock. 'Paralytic - sozzled - I believe one modern word is blootered.'

'I hadn't heard that one,' said Christopher, for some reason starting to feel almost normal, despite the weirdness of the conversation.

'So how did the police get involved?' said Jock. 'Did that Mr Browning stick his nose in again?'

'No, it wasn't him. They're not saying who it was, though.'

'I'll ask around,' said Jock, who was under the mistaken impression that he had contacts everywhere. In fact his only contacts were on the PLIF steering group and among the cleaning staff at his old school. On the other hand, maybe the cleaners would turn out to know what was going on, Christopher reflected. Jock had obtained some juicy titbits from them in his time.

'OK,' said Christopher. 'Have you seen Amaryllis?'

There was a pause.

'When, today?' said Jock.

'Well, yes,' said Christopher. So much had happened that it seemed ages since the day before - when quite a lot had happened too.

'No,' said Jock in the long-drawn-out way that sounded as if he might mean 'yes'. Or maybe he was just tantalising Christopher. 'Why?'

113

'No reason,' said Christopher. He wasn't sure why he had asked, except that he felt it might be useful to have Amaryllis on his side at the moment, even if only so that he could keep tabs on her and make sure she didn't do some way-out thing that would cause a lot more problems than it solved.

Just at that point the back of his neck tingled. He glanced round at the empty hall with the closed doors all round it - the police had shut the front door now - and then up the stairs to the top landing. And froze.

Amaryllis was waving and smiling at him from the top step.

'Got to go,' he said to Jock, slammed the phone down on its rest and tried to signal Amaryllis to go away. Evidently his semaphore didn't work, for she started to come down the stairs.

Christopher hurried to intercept her.

'What are you doing here?' he said in a low voice, halfway up the stairs, desperately hoping the policemen would all stay where they were. 'How the hell did you get in anyway?'

The first explanation that had popped into his head was that he had conjured her up just by thinking about her, but he told himself sternly not to be silly.

'I just thought you might need a bit of help,' she said, smiling at him. 'After all, you gave me a hand last night.'

Last night! Was it only last night he had battered in the panel under the sink in the old village hall and freed her from spider-infested captivity?

'You can't be seen up here!' said Christopher urgently. 'Hide in there - go on, hurry up!'

He more or less shoved her in through the door of the very small room he inhabited, usually only to sleep in it when he wasn't kept awake by noise from Caroline, shut the door behind her, turned away and then turned back momentarily, panicking about what she might find in there if she poked about a bit. Oh well, she had to find out sooner or later what a boring geek he was even if she didn't already know. He went back downstairs. Either she would wait meekly in there and he would let her out when the police had gone, or she wouldn't. He had very little control over it either way.

'What's going on up there?' said the first policeman, coming out of the sitting-room.

'Nothing,' lied Christopher. 'I just went up to see if I could find another game to play. Faisal keeps beating me at chess, so I thought I might have a better chance at Monopoly.'

Was that too much information? He held his breath.

'He's got that in here and he's already setting it up,' said the policeman, holding the door open for him. 'I'm not sure I'll have time to play though.'

He sounded quite wistful, as if he would have liked playing Monopoly to be in his job description.

'You could always start anyway,' said Christopher helpfully. 'Maybe Marina'll be back by the time you have to go.'

'I don't know that she'll be back any time soon,' said the policeman as they went into the sitting-room. 'She was last seen sitting by her mum's bedside weeping and wailing.'

'Oh, dear,' said Christopher. 'Sorry about that - I hope she isn't being too much of a pest.'

'It's not your fault,' said the policeman, giving him an odd look.

They started the game, and, predictably, the policeman had to leave just as he got a hotel on Old Kent Road, of which he was inordinately proud. The forensic team or whatever they were had finished in the kitchen, and Christopher and Faisal had the house to themselves. They had resumed the game, meticulously dividing up the policeman's assets between them, when Christopher suddenly remembered Amaryllis.

'Going to get you a jumper,' he said to Faisal, and climbed the stairs two at a time.

Amaryllis was deep in 'Now we are Six' - Christopher's childhood books were all sitting on a shelf above the computer.

'It's funny,' she said, waving the book at him, 'I never read these when I was younger. Didn't appeal at all. It's not bad, though. Quirky.'

'I'm in the middle of a game of Monopoly,' said Christopher. 'Just tell me what you're doing here.'

She shrugged her shoulders.

'I know who called the police.'

'Was it Mr Browning after all?'

'Who's that?.. No, it was your friend the customs officer.'

'Simon whatshisname? I had a talk with him earlier. He seemed all right.'

'I told you,' said Amaryllis, 'no such thing as a harmless bureaucrat.'

'How do you know he called the police?'

'I've been following him. I saw him talking to you this morning. I followed him after that.'

'But why would you bother?'

'It's just something I do. He came straight round to the end of this street and sat there in his car until the shouting and screaming started, and then called the police on his mobile and then drove off again. I waited a bit and then came in the bedroom window.'

'The bedroom window?' Christopher couldn't help saying, conscious that his part in this conversation had consisted almost entirely of short sharp questions in a querulous tone.

'Aren't you going to ask me why Simon Fairfax should call the police?' said Amaryllis.

'All right then, why should he?'

'He wants to get you into trouble so that he'll have a hold over you.'

'Get me into - ?' Christopher started to say, then stopped, reconsidered and said, 'I'm not in trouble, so he'll be disappointed, won't he?'

'Really?' she said, sounding sceptical. 'There aren't many people who would be so confident after what happened here.'

'I haven't done anything wrong,' he said. 'And what do you want with me anyway? What makes you think you can help me at all?'

'Well, I can play Monopoly,' she said, getting up from the swivel chair and putting 'Now we are Six' back on the shelf.

Chapter 9 Monopoly money

The rest of the evening was in its own way just as unbelievable as the day leading to it had been. Amaryllis joined in Monopoly with gusto, taking huge risks and plunging recklessly into property development, going bankrupt twice and apparently enjoying herself hugely. Faisal, who almost never spoke to strangers, came right out of his shell and had a long conversation with her about an obscure computer game which Christopher had banned him from having in the house on the grounds of extreme violence but which Caroline had nevertheless insisted on buying him for Christmas, and on which Amaryllis claimed to be an expert. She certainly knew a lot about weapons and their effects. More than a well-brought-up girl should know, said Christopher's inner old lady firmly.

As an uncle he felt he was just starting to make up for lost time. For just a few moments he looked at the world through rose-coloured spectacles and imagined the three of them as a proper family. He had to come down to earth when the phone rang.

'Mr Wilson?' said the anonymous voice on the other end. 'Mr Christopher Wilson?'

'Yes, speaking.'

'It's Kirkcaldy Memorial Hospital here. About your sister, Mrs Caroline Hussein.'

'Yes?'

'I'm afraid we're having to keep her in overnight. She's quite distraught.'

So what else is new? thought Christopher. 'Oh, dear,' he responded automatically.

'Yes, it has been very distressing for her daughter. Marina shouldn't really have had to witness this. We need somebody to take her home.'

'I'm sorry,' said Christopher, feeling useless again as he spoke. 'I'm looking after Caroline's son Faisal. I can't leave him on his own.'

'We need you to come in and collect Marina. She can't stay here.'

'Well, there isn't anybody else to - '

'You'll have to collect her before the end of evening visiting. There's nowhere for her to stay here.'

'But - '

'We're considering a psychiatric referral for Mrs Hussein. Your sister obviously needs help.'

The voice was reproachful. Christopher wanted to say, yes, I told the GP there were serious problems ages ago, and he didn't do anything then, so why is the NHS suddenly springing into action now, but he didn't. Instead he replied weakly, 'Thanks for letting me know. I'll be there as soon as I can but I don't have any transport....'

'I'll take you in the car,' said Amaryllis, suddenly appearing at his side. 'Faisal can come too - he might enjoy the ride.'

'Thanks,' he said, wondering if she would still be this keen to help once she had encountered the sullen Marina. He said to the hospital spokesperson, 'We'll be there in half an hour or so,' and rang off while the voice was still complaining about visiting times, people who were inconsiderate enough to live twenty miles from the nearest hospital and doubtless about other injustices he didn't have time to listen to.

So the three of them drove through the starry night over to Kirkcaldy to pick up Marina. Amaryllis was rather a scary person to be driven by - she seemed to think she was being followed everywhere, and would dive down side streets randomly as if in a chase scene from the movies. From the relative safety of the back seat, Faisal just laughed with excitement, while Christopher surreptitiously clung on to the passenger door pocket and hoped he wouldn't humiliate himself by being sick with fear.

Waiting on her own on a bench outside the main entrance, Marina didn't want to come with them; she did a very good impression of a child who was being molested by sinister strangers. Fortunately for Christopher, who had had enough drama for one day, all the passing health professionals studiously ignored her. He guessed that they had had enough of her and probably wouldn't have been too bothered if the Wyrd Sisters from Macbeth had arrived to take her away, as long as somebody did.

Once in Amaryllis's car, permitted to sit in the front seat as a special treat, as well as a treat for Christopher, who no longer flinched as they went round corners but was still in danger of embarrassing himself and everybody else by throwing up, Marina miraculously turned into a young girl again, apparently impressed by the sleek lines of the car's exterior, the dashboard resembling that of a jumbo jet, or just by Amaryllis's turn of speed.

Christopher felt his world had been turned on its head - almost literally as they cornered at sixty on the coast road between Kinghorn and Burntisland - by the day's events. Who would have thought Amaryllis would be so supportive in an emergency? From being some sort of ice woman she had turned into a model childminder, a perfect aunt.

He had been able to look in on Caroline briefly as she lay there, sedated, in one of these hospital gowns that drained all the colour from people's faces as well as robbing their bodies of all shape. There was a drip, and her hand was bandaged. Now that she was quiet and calm, he had a brief resurgence of brotherly affection.

'It's nice to see her so peaceful,' he commented to the nurse who came along to see if he wanted to ask anything.

'Yes, isn't it?' said the nurse grimly. 'It only took enough sedation to knock out an elephant, too.'

'Oh, dear,' he said.

She put a hand on his arm.

'This is for the best, Mr Wilson. I expect you've been through the mill with her.'

'Sort of,' he admitted. 'Will they keep her in?'

'She could get transferred tomorrow,' said the nurse. 'To ERI or Ninewells maybe. We'll let you know.'

'Thank you.'

Christopher wasn't sure how much to tell the children - how much they might have worked out for themselves - but as they went in the front door at home Marina said, 'They're sending her to another hospital, aren't they? A special one.'

'I hope they keep her there,' said Faisal.

'No!' said Marina. 'I hope they make her better and send her home.'

'I think that's what they're hoping too,' said Christopher. He was willing Amaryllis to stay and not to feel she should leave them alone to get on with it. Fortunately she didn't seem to be the kind of person who used sensitivity as an excuse for inaction, and she organised and played two more games of Monopoly before Marina and Faisal went to bed. After that she left, pleading tiredness - so why did he picture her prowling about in the night like a sleek pale cat, playing games with the darkness?

He didn't sleep much that night. The events of the day replayed themselves on a repeating loop, sometimes in slow motion, sometimes on fast forward, mostly in black and white and occasionally in colour. Even when he played chess with Faisal he had a limited amount of control over the pieces, but in real life he was a pawn in a bigger game played on a larger board by someone as yet unseen, for he didn't think either Simon Fairfax or Amaryllis was actually controlling him, although it had seemed like that at times over the past few days.

During Sunday morning, as he read the paper with very little attention to any of the stories, a nurse phoned him from Kirkcaldy and asked him to come into the hospital. It would be a hellish journey on a Sunday, but the request was peremptory, more of an order really. He didn't know what to do about Marina and Faisal. He knew if he took them with him, they would be completely impossible en route, whether the small party travelled by train or bus – they would complain about the journey, they would want to go to the toilet when there was no toilet, they would want to gorge themselves on luminous sweets until they were physically ill, and want Diet Coke when there was only Pepsi, and Pepsi Max when there was only Coca Cola. Anyway, he didn't know what sort of situation was waiting at the hospital. It was possible - though it didn't seem very likely, in view of what had been said about psychiatric assessment - that they were about to discharge Caroline. It was equally possible that she had become very much worse and not fit for the children to see. He couldn't leave them at home on their own. There were no friends he could call on. Mr Browning was completely out of the question as a babysitter. He couldn't ask Amaryllis to step in again – in spite of the events of the previous day, he hardly knew her, after all. She could still be a serial killer, even though he and the children got on well with her.

The door-bell rang.

It was Jock McLean. Christopher could have hugged him if he hadn't known Jock's extremely politically incorrect views on men hugging each other. Jock would be the ideal person to leave with the kids.

'I'm going over to my son's at Milngavie this morning,' Jock said, unwittingly squashing Christopher's urge to hug. 'Just wanted to let you know I won't be at the PLIF meeting tonight.'

'PLIF meeting?'

'Aye, it's the regular monthly meeting at the Queen of Scots, not one of your extraordinary meetings in the Elgin Arms - comes round quickly, doesn't it? Time passes...'

Jock gave a great sigh.

'I've got to go over to Kirkcaldy,' said Christopher. 'Caroline's still in hospital.'

'Oh, I'm sorry to hear that... Some journey, too, with the kids. Dear, oh dear.'

Jock shook his head sorrowfully and refrained from offering help. He made a quick getaway after that.

The phone rang.

'I can't make it to the PLIF meeting tonight,' said Young Dave abruptly, as was his style. 'Got to go and see the wife's mother. She's worrying about something or other to do with her pension - typical! Don't know why she can't save the worrying for the last Friday of the month when the wife goes round there to do the recycling.'

'Well, if you're worried, you're worried,' said Christopher nonsensically.

Another one down. He wondered if Big Dave and Mrs Stevenson would be next, more rats deserting the sinking ship. He might have to cancel the meeting anyway, since he had no idea how long this thing at the hospital would take. Probably better to cancel now, in fact. He had lifted the receiver to call Big Dave when the door-bell rang again. For goodness' sake, it was like Waverley Station in here.

'Everything all right?' said Big Dave, looming reassuringly on the doorstep. 'I heard there was a bit of trouble.'

'Yes,' said Christopher. 'It's Caroline - she's in hospital. I've got to get over there today and speak to the doctor.'

'Kirkcaldy?' said Big Dave.

'Yes. But they might be transferring her later on. I was just wondering what to do about the kids.'

He looked past Big Dave - quite a tricky feat in itself - and saw a very large white van outside the house.

'I'll take you all over there now in the van if you want,' said Big Dave. He brushed aside any attempt to thank him, apparently embarrassed to have caused gratitude to be felt. Once they were at the hospital, he kept Marina and Faisal in the van with him while Christopher went in for the confrontation with the doctor. There were sweets in the van, and as Christopher got out, Big Dave was starting a game of I-spy with Faisal. Marina had of course plugged herself into her iPod on leaving the house and, if past experience was anything to go by, wouldn't disconnect until the battery ran down.

Christopher half-expected them to discharge Caroline without warning and leave him to provide transport and nursing care on the spur of the moment - in fact, he was pleasantly surprised that they hadn't yet dumped her on his doorstep with a label tied round her neck - but on this occasion they seemed to have taken things seriously, and he returned to Big Dave's van with the news that she would probably be transferred to a psychiatric bed as soon as possible, and that she might be in hospital for some time. 'Then there's the liver situation,' one of the doctors had commented cryptically. 'There's no knowing how that's going to play out.'

'It's all for the best,' said Big Dave. 'Do you give up yet?'

Apparently the question was directed to Faisal, although Christopher felt it might well have been aimed at him.

'I'm going to have to cancel the PLIF meeting tonight,' he said to Big Dave on the drive home. 'Jock's gone to Milngavie and Young Dave rang up with a sob-story about his mother-in-law's pension.'

Big Dave sighed. 'And there was me and Mrs Stevenson looking forward to it,' he said. Christopher couldn't tell whether he was joking or not.

'And weren't we going to do anything about the Midsummer Party?' he added.

'Oh, yes, I think we were,' said Christopher. 'But it won't be any use if we don't have a quorum.'

'What about the lassie?'

'Amaryllis? She isn't strictly speaking on the steering group.'

'This is no time to be abiding strictly by the rules,' said Big Dave darkly. 'Jock McLean and Young Dave won't be missed. The rest of us can work out a strategy without them... Mrs Stevenson's quite a strategic thinker, you know. Hidden depths, that woman.'

Christopher's mind boggled.

'All right,' he said reluctantly. 'But it'll have to be at the house, not in the Queen of Scots. I can't leave Marina and Faisal on their own.'

He ruthlessly squashed the guilt he now felt at having left them with Caroline so often when, as he now realised, her drinking had caused her to become unstable and violent. He couldn't do anything about that now except to try and be a better parent than she had ever been. The vague idea that someone, such as a social worker, might now come along who wouldn't give him the chance to be a parent or even an uncle, crossed his mind, leaving him more shaken than he had been at any time during this crisis.

'I'll bring a carry-out,' said Big Dave happily. 'And Mrs Stevenson. You can let Amaryllis know. Eight o'clock all right with you?'

When Big Dave dropped them off at the house, Christopher looked at his watch and realised it was around lunch-time - he had imagined it to be much later. He felt so tired that he would happily have gone back to bed, instead of having to play several more games of Monopoly with Faisal, who seemed reluctant to return to his usual splendid isolation and the comfort of killing aliens on his Playstation.

By tea-time, Christopher was seriously starting to flag when a voice said from the sitting-room doorway,

'Fish 'n' chips anybody?'

It was of course Amaryllis, bearing the gift of three fish suppers with onion rings on the side. Faisal greeted her like an old friend and Marina graciously agreed to come downstairs and eat for once.

'Monopoly money,' said Amaryllis, dreamily running the contents of the bank through her fingers as they ate all round the room, contravening previously enforced house rules. She herself insisted she had already eaten, and certainly to judge from her figure fish and chips would never have been on the menu in any home of hers. 'That's what we need.'

'Monopoly money?' said Christopher through a particularly big chip. Oh, God, I'm doing it again, he thought. 'Sorry, I didn't mean to keep doing that. Repeating what you say, I mean. I've been trying not to… What do we need it for? Oh, the village hall, I suppose.'

'Yes, among other things,' said Amaryllis. He wondered idly if she was planning to rob a bank or if she just really liked playing games. Both, possibly.

'How did you get into the house?' said Faisal suddenly, folding up his fish and chip paper and then rolling into a ball.

'I've got a way,' said Amaryllis.

'Does that mean burglars could get in that way too?'

'Only if they had special training,' replied Amaryllis.

Christopher started to feel very uneasy. He had been trying not to think about this ever since his conversation with Simon Fairfax the day before. But now that Faisal had mentioned the word 'burglars' he wasn't sure he could help mulling it over. Which side of the law was Amaryllis on? And was she always been on the same side or did her loyalties change with the wind? He didn't want to think badly of her after the help she had given him but she did have certain skills that would have been very useful to someone who was up to no good.

'Are you staying for the meeting?' he asked politely to take his mind off the other things.

'Meeting?'

'There's a PLIF steering group meeting tonight. I've asked them to come here for it. Young Dave and Jock McLean won't be here though.'

'Another meeting already? It only seems like - well, a day or two - since the last one.'

'The last one was an extraordinary meeting. We've gone over to regular weekly meetings now because of the emergency.'

'Have you ever thought that you might be taking this meetings thing a bit too far?' Amaryllis enquired, still clutching several five hundred pound notes from the Monopoly bank. 'They must be taking up all your spare time.'

'You can't have too many meetings,' Christopher muttered. 'It's democracy in action.'

'That isn't what you said when you came home the other night,' Faisal pointed out. 'I heard you on the landing swearing about meetings. You said meetings were - '

'Thanks, Faisal, I don't think everybody in the world needs to know what I said. I was over-tired and – ''

'And over-emotional,' said Marina. Christopher felt his jaw drop. He couldn't remember the last time Marina had even attempted to bandy words with him and Faisal in the way that, until he actually had a family living with him, he had fondly imagined ideal families would do. She almost sounded as if she had been listening and taking in what was going on, and not as if she inhabited a faraway place that nobody else could reach. For almost the first time since Christopher had met her, she seemed like the kind of person it would be worthwhile taking an interest in, encouraging and -

Christopher once again deliberately stopped his thoughts in their tracks. He didn't want to get too interested in what happened to those two children, in case they were effectively kidnapped by the authorities in the wake of their mother's departure. If he didn't care too much, he wouldn't feel so desperate on the day the social workers came in and took them – that was the theory, anyway.

He had to go out of the room for a while then, pretending to gather up the fish and chip papers and put them in the bin, but actually standing in the kitchen and trying to stop himself breaking down.

Big Dave and Mrs Stevenson arrived soon after that, restoring normality by looking and behaving very much as they always did, and soon the sitting-room had turned into a rough approximation of a PLIF meeting venue. Christopher, almost always a stickler for procedure, felt somehow reluctant to pursue the usual agenda at this small and strange meeting, and they sat in easy chairs, drinking, staring out between the curtains at the dark garden, and talking inconsequentially.

The door-bell rang again. Christopher jumped, realising in that moment that the picture of the social workers dragging Marina and Faisal screaming down the garden path had been lurking just under the surface in his mind. He glanced quickly round like a cornered animal looking for a hiding place.

'You all right, son?' said Big Dave, who was probably not old enough to be Christopher's father but who often took a quasi paternal interest in him nevertheless.

'Yes, fine,' said Christopher, taking a deep breath. Amaryllis was also observing him closely.

He went to the front door.

A strange man stood on the doorstep with a package that looked very much like fish and chips. Christopher peered at it.

'Fish and chips?' he said, feeling stupid.

'I think you dropped this outside in the street,' said the man, perhaps an American, handing the package to Christopher.

Christopher sniffed at it cautiously. It smelled of salt and vinegar.

'Fish and chips?' he said again.

'I don't think so,' said the American.

'I don't want it,' said Christopher, trying to hand it back. He had a lingering sense of danger, as if perhaps the package contained an explosive device, or a quantity of drugs which would later be used to frame him, or.....

The American refused to take it back. He pushed it at Christopher. 'Open it,' he said.

'No,' said Christopher clearly. 'I don't want this and I want you off my doorstep. Now.'

Putting forty odd years of upbringing and restraint behind him, he closed the door in the man's face.

The door-bell rang again a few times, but he refused to open the door, standing instead in the hall with his arms folded and a smug little smile on his face. Then there was a different sound, and the package appeared, rather squashed, on its way through the letter-box. Christopher tried to push it back out again, but it resisted - the flap was only designed to work one way, evidently, although he had never thought of that before - and eventually it fell in an untidy heap on the door-mat. He gathered up the messy package with a sigh and carried it through to the kitchen, where he planned to throw it straight in the kitchen bin. He didn't really care at this point if it did contain a bomb or millions of pounds worth of cocaine, he just wanted to get it out of the way. As he put it down on the kitchen table, the wrapping fell apart.

There was a large amount of money in hundred pound notes.

Amaryllis chose that moment to make an entrance through the door from the sitting-room.

'Monopoly money!' she said with glee.

The kitchen was suddenly full of people: the lure of money had drawn in Big Dave and Mrs Stevenson, and had brought Marina and Faisal down from upstairs. They all stood around the table marvelling like shepherds clustered around the baby Jesus.

Chapter 10 Root of all evil?

'Damn!' said Christopher. 'I forgot to ask him if he knew Maisie Sue - '

'There must be thousands here!' said Big Dave.

Mrs Stevenson said nothing: perhaps she was silently mulling over how many new woolly hats or Dubonnets and lemonade she could buy with all that money.

'But why?' said Christopher helplessly.

Marina sniffed at the ruined package.

'Yuck,' she said, 'it smells of old fish and chips.'

'You could get a lot of Playstation games with that,' said Faisal greedily.

'Who gave you it? What do they expect in return?' said Amaryllis, eyes sharp and watchful.

'He didn't say. Sounded a bit American to me, but I'm no use at accents. But he was pretty determined I should have it. He shoved it through the letter-box when I wouldn't take it.'

'Maybe there was somebody taking photographs,' suggested Mrs Stevenson. 'Maybe it's some kind of a sting.'

'I hope there was somebody taking photographs,' said Christopher. 'They'll have seen this man behaving like a complete idiot. Pushing fish and chips through my letter-box - it isn't the act of a rational man, is it?'

'But what if you get caught with the money?' persisted Mrs Stevenson. 'How are you going to explain it?'

'It isn't up to me to explain it!' said Christopher. 'Anyway, I'm not going to get caught with it. I'm taking it straight round to the police station.'

As if someone had been waiting for their cue, a thunderous knocking suddenly resounded round the house.

'Police! Open up!'

'Oh, for God's sake,' said Christopher.

'Quick, hide the money!' said Amaryllis. 'In the oven. Then if they search the house and find it, you can claim you were just re-heating a fish supper.'

'That's criminal in itself,' said Big Dave. 'Shouldn't be allowed. Fish and chips should be eaten - '

'Out of the way!' said Christopher, pushing past him to get to the oven as the thunderous knocking continued. He shoved the package on to the middle shelf. 'Should I turn the heat on?'

'Only if you want the fire brigade here as well as the police,' said Amaryllis. 'I've got to go now. I can't be seen here.'

She disappeared abruptly. Christopher opened the door. Finding the police on his doorstep twice in two days was a bit much, he reflected as they rushed in to search the house. At least they wouldn't find a woman covered in blood in the kitchen this time - unless Mrs Stevenson had gone haywire with one of the knives in an attempt to divert their attention.

They searched everywhere except in the oven. It was almost as if they were deliberately avoiding it. Christopher asked one of them what they expected to find, but predictably there was no answer. Eventually they told him not to leave town for the next few days - chance would be a fine thing! - and left again empty-handed. Christopher decided that for reasons only known to himself, the American had tipped them off, this time having planted evidence - of what? - in the house. Perhaps he was connected with Simon Fairfax, whose determination to get Christopher into trouble was almost comical, but Christopher found it sinister as well - and he sincerely hoped it would backfire sooner or later. He wished Amaryllis had stayed on.

'So - what are you going to do with the money?' said Mrs Stevenson, eyes gleaming.

'I don't think we'd better talk about the money,' said Christopher. 'What if they've bugged the place?'

'We could talk about it in the shower,' said Marina.

'In the shower?' said Christopher.

'With the water running - they can't hear through the noise,' Faisal explained.

'You've been watching too many thrillers on TV,' said Mrs Stevenson, trying to twinkle at them and succeeding in looking like the scary old witch from 'Hansel and Gretel'. They reacted by stepping back from her slightly. Christopher covered up for them by saying,

'Anyway, I still think I should hand the money in to the police.'

'Why can't we spend it?' said Faisal wistfully.

'I think you know why we can't,' said Christopher gently.

'Because it doesn't belong to us,' Marina told her brother, not at all gently. 'Stupid!'

'OK, this is what I'm going to do next,' said Christopher. It wouldn't do any harm to have Big Dave and Mrs Stevenson as witnesses to his good intentions. 'I'm going to post it to the police without any covering note saying who it's from. Then it'll be their problem, not mine.'

'What about fingerprints?' said Marina, who seemed to be shaping up for a career in crime or detection herself.

'And DNA,' added Faisal, not to be outdone. They had definitely been watching too many thrillers somewhere along the line.

'Oh, for goodness' sake,' said Christopher, starting to feel very tired.

'You could put gloves on and wrap it up differently,' suggested Mrs Stevenson.

It was agreed that they would all put on gloves and help, so that they were all equally implicated. Christopher wished Amaryllis could be implicated in this operation too - he found himself unnerved every time she came into and left his house apparently at will. He had scanned the outside walls for any handholds, and as far as he could tell there were none. The roof was steeply pitched and high above the ground; he couldn't see how she could reach it, although there was a skylight in the attic through which someone of her slim build might have been able to slither.

Big Dave offered to pass the finished parcel on to Young Dave to post in Dunfermline, without telling him what the contents were. Christopher, usually a bit of a loner, realised he was no longer panicking quite as much as if he had been working through this completely on his own. The weekend had been a revelation in that respect as well as in several others.

As he handed the parcel - now held together with duck tape and looking rather different from the ramshackle package it had been when the American first pushed it through the letterbox - to Big Dave, Christopher had the uneasy feeling that he hadn't seen the last of it, but he dismissed this as the vague imaginings of an overwrought mind. Surely this weird weekend must be over now.

Big Dave and Mrs Stevenson hesitated on their way out.

'Would you have liked us to stay the night?' said Big Dave suddenly.

Christopher was too taken aback to reply.

'We don't like to leave you on your own,' said Mrs Stevenson, adding coyly, 'We wouldn't take up much space - we could always share the settee.'

Christopher hoped his jaw hadn't dropped; he certainly felt he had been given far too much information. Big Dave nodded serenely.

'Thought you might like the company.'

'It's very kind of you - '

'There you are, David, I knew he wanted us to stay!' said Mrs Stevenson excitedly.

'You were right, Jemima,' said Big Dave, blushing slightly - although why he should blush when revealing that he knew Mrs Stevenson's first name, Christopher wasn't sure, when so much else had been revealed.

Suddenly he had to get out of the house.

He realised that now that Big Dave and Mrs Stevenson, whom he knew he would always think of her by that name and never as Jemima, were determined to stay, he could abandon Marina and Faisal to their care, and go for a proper walk, making up for the one that had been interrupted the day before by Simon Fairfax. It was an enticing thought, seeing the river by moonlight, being on his own again, with the opportunity to forget all the various things that had disturbed his composure over the weekend. It wasn't even that late in the day.

He gave Big Dave and Mrs Stevenson strict instructions to call him on his mobile if anything happened at all. He even took the trouble to switch on his mobile, something he rarely did, although it was a pity he then left it on the hall table. He didn't realise that was what he had done until he was walking down the road that led to the river. He didn't cast a sideways glance at Merchantman Wynd this time, afraid of conjuring up a dark monster from the shadows. It was a lovely evening, and everything went just as he had imagined: the reflections of lights on the river, the joy of not having any background noise, the forgetting....

That part didn't go according to plan at all

He was almost at the harbour when it happened, in a quiet street where tasteful cottage style houses had been built in the 1920s, each one with a sizeable front garden. They must have bulldozed whole terraces of traditional fishermen's dwellings to do this.

Christopher had paused to admire the hydrangeas in pots outside someone's front door when something buzzed past him. He blinked in surprise. Unusual for a bee to fly about at this time of night. Maybe it was a very small bat. For no reason he suddenly noticed, right in the middle of this thought, that his shoes felt loose. Had he lost weight without noticing it, or were the laces coming undone? He paused under a lamp-post and bent to check, leaning down further to re-fasten the looser lace.

Something pinged against the wrought-iron stem of the lamp-post, one of the few remaining examples of Victorian street furniture in the town. He straightened and glanced round to see if anyone was throwing stones. He didn't share Jock McLean's hostility towards teenagers, but there were always some -

Suddenly a blow landed right between his shoulders, pushing him down. He fell forward on to the strip of grass between the kerb and the pavement. He landed on hands and knees; the shock of impact travelled up to his elbows and shoulders. Then came a second blow in the middle of his back, and an angry voice with an American accent not far away: 'Get down! Get down and stay down, for Christ's sake!'

He flattened himself on the grass verge, not even daring to turn his head to find out what was happening. He wanted to close his eyes, but forced himself not to.

Another ping from the lamp-post. Running footsteps on the road surface. A dull thud quite close to him, a cut-off yelp from across the street.

'Got him!' grunted the American. Christopher felt a hand on his shoulder.

'Hey you - get back there in the garden! - don't stand up - don't come out until I give the word.'

Christopher was in no mood to argue. Half-crouching, he scurried into the nearest garden, which fortunately had a rather impressive beech hedge in full leaf for him to hide behind. The leaves would probably be an attractive green-gold colour in daylight at this time of year.

He hadn't worked out what was going on yet, but he still didn't feel safe. What if there were gunmen in the house behind him, just waiting for the chance to emerge and shoot him in the back? What if the American who had spoken to him wasn't really on his side at all?

He peered through the gaps in the beech leaves. Something was happening across the road. A tall figure leaned down to look at a dark shape on the ground – reached down and grabbed hold and then dragged it along. A body? Horror and curiosity vied with each other as he pushed the leaves aside to get a better view.

'Just you stay right where you are. I'm calling the police,' said a man's voice somewhere behind him. He was somewhat reassured by the robust local accent.

'Wait a minute. Is he all right?' said another voice, a woman, also with a strong West Fife accent. Somebody came up behind him and touched the side of his head tentatively. There was an indrawing of breath. 'That's blood on him,' she added. 'Better call an ambulance too.' She withdrew, her steps padding like those of an animal.

Christopher turned his head. He didn't think it was blood. He must have got his face wet lying on the grass verge. He put a hand up to touch his face, and then looked at the darkish stain in alarm. It was blood. What exactly was going on here? Had he been shot?

He turned round. Two middle-aged people were watching him from the doorway of the house. The woman was wearing fluffy slippers and a dressing-gown.

'It's all right,' he said. When he turned his head back to look at the scene in the street, he could see nothing of the man dragging the body; everything had gone quiet. It was as if he had imagined it all - apart from the blood.

The man shook his head. 'Vandals throwing stones,' he said. He turned away. 'Come away in, Madge. I'm calling the police now, for all the good it'll do.'

'What about the blood?' said Madge to Christopher. 'Are you sure you're not hurt, dear?'

'I'm fine,' said Christopher, trying to smile reassuringly. She shook her head too, and followed the man into the house.

Christopher didn't want to leave the sanctuary of the garden, where life seemed more or less normal, and go out to the street again, but he had no choice. He had to get out of the way before the police turned up: they would undoubtedly take him in for questioning if they came across him again today. He headed on down towards the harbour, ignoring trembling legs and morbid thoughts.

Just after he passed the Elgin Arms, a car drew up. He paused. Simon Fairfax wound down the passenger window. Visions of abandoned mineshafts flooded back into Christopher's mind; being shot at and then kidnapped within half an hour would be the perfect end to an insane day.

'What are you doing here?' he said to Simon.

'I was going to offer you a lift home - thought you might be glad of it,' said Simon ingenuously.

'Ha!' said Christopher. 'Well, I'm not. Glad, I mean.'

'Why not?'

'I'm not getting in any strange cars today.'

'It's perfectly safe.'

'Do you know anything about - all this?' said Christopher.

'Don't know what you're talking about,' said Simon.

They exchanged stares. Christopher didn't know what to make of Simon's bland demeanour.

What about the money?' he said at last.

'What money?' said Simon. His surprise seemed genuine enough.

'So you don't know anything about the shooting or about the money?'

'I'm afraid not. Of course, I would have given a hand if I'd been passing... No, you need to look further afield. Much further. There are people involved in this who you probably haven't even thought of. Now, do you want a lift home or not?'

Christopher was getting bored with being people talking in riddles. He shrugged, turned and walked away. He wasn't planning to engage in any more pointless conversations until he heard something a bit more convincing. For all he knew, Amaryllis could be working

140

with Simon Fairfax to drive him insane without any other mysterious strangers being involved at all. He wasn't going to believe anyone or worry about anything from now on, until someone came up with a good reason why he should.

His determination lasted until he drew level with the small block of apartments in Merchantman Wynd, glanced up and saw Amaryllis looking down at him from her balcony.

'Come on up,' she called softly.

'You're not going to offer me a laced cocktail and then spirit me away to Morocco as a white slave, are you?' It was a long complex thought by Christopher's standards, but it just came sliding out of his mouth as if he had rehearsed it until he was word-perfect.

'No, of course not.'

'In that case I can't possibly come up,' he said, and walked on.

He arrived home without further incident, although walking in on Big Dave and Mrs Stevenson in each other's arms on the settee was enough to convince him that the weirdness of the weekend definitely wouldn't be over until the fat lady sang. He didn't know whether Jemima Stevenson could sing or not, and sincerely hoped he would never find out.

Chapter 11 The morning after the weird weekend

Finding Big Dave and Mrs Stevenson ensconsed in the kitchen presiding over breakfast when you got up in the morning was enough to make anyone wish they had had a long lie. Much as Christopher liked both of them, he would never have dreamed of asking them to stay the night, and certainly not together, perish the thought squire. He wished people would stay in the pigeon holes where he had put them, and not hop around from one to another, bringing chaos and confusion in their wake. If only he could have assigned either Amaryllis or Simon to an appropriate pigeon-hole, he felt his life might have been quite a lot simpler at this point. But he just didn't think he had a suitable place to put them, since he had never met anyone like either of them, and had never even conjured them up in his imagination either.

Christopher slid into a chair and with a fairly good grace accepted an offer of dark brown tea from Mrs Stevenson. He doubted if he had the energy even to brew himself a cup after a restless night during which he re-lived the bee buzzing past and the determined shove between the shoulders several times. And he kept thinking there were spots of blood dotted over his hands, his shirt, his face, the banisters, the bathroom mirror, even now on the table in front of him. He rubbed at an imaginary spot just in front of his tea cup.

'There isn't any blood,' said Big Dave. 'Who do you think you are? – Lady Macbeth?'

He and Mrs Stevenson hadn't shown any surprise at Christopher's appearance the previous evening, and had helped him to decide to have a shower and put his clothes in the wash, not exactly bullying him into these decisions but not letting him do anything else. They had made him drink far too many cups of the extra strong tea, but with lots of sugar 'for the shock', and Big Dave had had to restrain Mrs Stevenson from personally supervising Christopher in the shower, a memory that made him cringe. He thought he might have to be eternally grateful to them, a burden he didn't much want to bear.

He noticed the parcel wasn't on the kitchen table.

'Have you posted it already?' he commented casually. 'I didn't know the Post Office was open this early.'

'We thought you'd taken it out to post,' said Mrs Stevenson – he didn't think he would ever be able to think of her as Jemima, no matter how many times she followed him into the shower.

'Has it gone?'

Oddly, Christopher's first reaction to the disappearance of the parcel of money was one of jubilation: he wouldn't have to deal with the money or any of the repercussions himself, it was now officially someone else's problem. Unfortunately just as it lumbered out of the starting blocks, this first comforting reaction was overtaken by a different, altogether more alarming one. What if Amaryllis had taken the parcel? No, rephrase that: Amaryllis must have taken the parcel. It was just the kind of thing she would do, entering the house in the middle of the night by the secret entrance, the location of which Christopher still couldn't quite pin down, and stealing the wrapped up wads of cash from right under their noses. She was probably on the way to the airport right now to fly off somewhere exotic and do something indescribably evil with the money.

No, wait a minute. She had probably been stopped on her way to the airport by a secret government organisation of which only two people in the country were aware, and taken to an abandoned mineshaft somewhere to moulder away until -

No. Wait another minute. Amaryllis had obviously swanned off with the money - not to do something dreadful, but to live in luxury for the rest of her life in a secret hiding place where nobody could track her down again. For at least two minutes Christopher could feel nothing apart from envy. He wasn't bothered one way or another about the luxury, but not being tracked down sounded like an extremely attractive option.

Being tracked down... excavating a little among all the envy he discovered a tiny sensation of disquiet. What if she had shared the secret of the parcel with Simon Fairfax and was even now in the shiny black car on her way to the abandoned mineshaft? Christopher's conscience was rather overdeveloped, possibly as a result of always having had to look after a younger and more unruly sibling. Somehow he couldn't bring himself to shrug this off and ignore the danger Amaryllis had placed herself in, which he had to admit was partly as a result of his careless attitude to the parcel of money from the start. He should either have handed it over to the police when they had searched the house - although he had secretly enjoyed the suspense of wondering if they would stumble on it themselves - or, failing that, he should have tried to use one of these bank night safes he had often seen but didn't really understand, or even gone to the bus station and put the parcel in a locker - if the lockers were still open, which knowing bus stations and the facilities therein, they probably weren't. Anyway, it was too late to start worrying about bus stations now.

On the other hand, he could at least see if Amaryllis was all right. Sighing at the idea of skipping breakfast - especially as Big Dave and Mrs Stevenson had pushed the boat out and cooked the dodgy-looking kippers they had found at the back of the freezer - he slurped his tea and set out to save her. Or not, as the case might be.

He wished, as he hurried back along the road and down the street leading to the harbour, then round the corner to Merchantman Wynd with its odd associations, that he had been modern enough to exchange mobile numbers with the woman. It would have saved quite a bit of leg work. It would be interesting to see, though, the next time he summoned up the interest to step on the bathroom scales, if all this exercise had kept his weight down, or if that would be counterbalanced by the increased intake of fish and chips. Christopher wasn't really too bothered either way.

Where was her flat again? Everything looked different in daylight. He wondered if he had dreamed seeing her the night before? No, he hadn't, because there she was again, sitting on the balcony of the uncharacteristically upmarket little block of apartments. The windows at the other side of the building must have a great view across the Forth on a clear day. Even a misty day would have its own charms, he supposed. This Monday morning the weather was neither one thing nor the other - lots of greyish-white clouds about, no rain yet, no sign of blue sky.

'Amaryllis!' he called as softly as possible, so as not to attract attention.

She didn't look up from her newspaper. He tried again. When she still didn't move, Christopher had a couple of very scary moments, imagining that Simon

Fairfax, or indeed one of the other dangerous people who had suddenly appeared in Pitkirtly, had killed her and left her propped up in the corner of the balcony with a coffee cup in her hand.

She glanced up.

'Christopher!'

He couldn't tell whether she was pleased to see him or not.

'I'm still not offering to take you to Tunisia as a white slave,' she said with a grin.

'Morocco.'

'Do you want to come up? Or will I come down?'

'Have you got the parcel?' said Christopher urgently.

'The what?'

'The parcel!' He was about to elaborate when he noticed that one of the neighbours had appeared on an adjoining balcony, watering-can at the ready, obviously intent on listening to the conversation while pretending to water his hanging baskets. 'Too obvious, idiot,' muttered Christopher. He didn't usually mutter to himself quite so much, or call people idiots for that matter, but circumstances had driven him to it.

'Go to the front door and I'll buzz you in,' she said, surreptitiously pointing at the man with the watering-can.

Christopher had been right: the view from the front room was amazing. You could even see the Forth Bridges if you craned your neck in the right direction. Looking the other way, the familiar shapes of Longannet Power Station and the Grangemouth oil refinery were far enough away to enhance the landscape rather than being blots on it.

The apartment was fairly empty and basic. He guessed that she didn't want it to reveal anything about her personality.

'So – are you going to tell me about last night?' said Amaryllis, coming in from the balcony and leaning on the living room door frame.

'Last night?'

'No need to put on that innocent expression for me, Christopher Wilson,' she said, and he saw the primary school teacher in her for the first time. 'Shots fired in one of those boring street further down the town - and then you come casually round the corner spattered with blood and - '

'How did you know?'

'I know shots when I hear them,' she said. 'And I saw you. You were out of it. Something bad happened. You thought you needed me but you didn't. You needed to go straight home and get Jemima Stevenson to make you ten cups of tea with sugar.'

'Are you psychic or what?' snapped Christopher. He suddenly found his legs weren't supporting him very effectively. He glanced round wildly for somewhere to sit down. Amaryllis took a step away from the door frame and pushed a wooden chair towards him. He grabbed it, held it still to make sure it wouldn't slide out from under him, and sank into it.

'Or what,' she said.

'What's that supposed to mean?'

'I'm not psychic, I just have more experience than most people of tricky situations that involve guns, so I know shots when I hear them. I know the after-effects and the glazed look innocent bystanders get when they survive something like that... I'm not proud of it. It's just what's happened in my life.'

He stared at her. 'What does it all mean? Why is it happening here? Those things don't happen in Pitkirtly.'

'I don't know yet... Did you see anybody you recognised?'

'Only Simon Fairfax, but that was afterwards. He wasn't involved in it.'

'How can you be sure?'

'I can't be. You know that!' He couldn't help a note of exasperation entering his voice. She should know by now that he was just an innocent bystander in all this.

'So what's this about a parcel?' said Amaryllis coolly and calmly.

'The parcel with - you know what - in it.'

'Parcel? Oh - the fish and chips!'

'We decided it would be best to re-wrap it and post it to the police anonymously,' he said, feeling obscurely proud of this simple little plan.

'Yes, that sounds like the kind of thing you would do,' she replied, squashing the pride completely flat.

'What do you mean?'

'Well, it's a good idea but what about fingerprints? and DNA?'

'The kids said that too.... We wore gloves.'

'Hmm,' said Amaryllis.

'So - have you got it?'

'Who - me?'

'Yes, of course you. Who else would sneak into the house and take it in the middle of the night without so much as a by-your-leave?'

'I don't know,' said Amaryllis. 'But it definitely wasn't me. Are you absolutely sure it isn't still in the house?'

He thought about it.

'Big Dave and Mrs Stevenson haven't seen it. And the kids didn't say anything.'

'Didn't say anything?' she said sceptically. 'Isn't that a bit suspicious?'

'Not really. They don't say a lot normally. Well, except for Marina arguing with Caroline, that is.'

'Is there anything you're not telling me about this parcel?' she demanded suddenly, after searching his face with those grey-blue eyes, hard as marbles and almost as swirly.

'No - um, yes,' he said. Her denial rang true - not that he was the best person to detect lies, in fact quite the contrary. 'Simon Fairfax.'

'Simon Fairfax gave you the parcel?'

'No, a different man gave me it. He might have been American, but I'm no good at accents. It was Simon Fairfax who told me it was bugged.'

'Bugged?'

'Yes, you know, with bugs - the kind of thing the security service uses. For tracking.'

'Tracking... ' She laughed.

'So you definitely haven't got it?'

'Definitely not. Wouldn't touch it with a barge-pole. Simon Fairfax must be slipping.'

For a moment those eyes looked into the middle distance at something he didn't want to know about, and then they re-focussed on him. She was smiling rather unpleasantly.

'We could try turning it back on him, of course,' she said slowly.

'What do you mean?'

'We could bug this other man. The American. And I mean really bug him. He'd be furious.'

'But how - ?'

Christopher felt as if he was trapped in an odd and slightly surreal game where he could only ask questions - and only silly ones at that - and Amaryllis would never give him a straight answer, but he was supposed to work out what was going on. It was like going to the cinema with the Delphic Oracle.

She went to a desk in the corner of the living-room and unlocked a drawer. He half-expected her to bring out a Colt 45 or similar weapon; he was convinced she must have worked in the police - maybe even Special Branch if it still existed - or possibly still did. He hoped it was nothing more sinister than that.

She brought out a very slim envelope, which she put in her handbag.

'Ask no questions and you'll be told no lies,' she said to Christopher cryptically. 'Let's go.'

Chapter 12 Bugs

In a way it was incongruous that she carried a handbag at all - he found himself examining it as they went along to see if he could spot any secret compartments or places where you might carry a gun, just as in some handbags he had noticed a place for an umbrella. But it looked like a perfectly normal bag, albeit rather larger than current fashion dictated. More like a small rucksack really - which would be useful if her route took her over the rooftops or through skylights, he supposed.

'Do you think the American had something to do with what happened last night?' he asked, just to avoid an awkward silence.

There was an uneasy pause.

'Do you know anything about him?' he persisted.

'Could be,' she said.

They walked up the road, heading, he presumed, back towards his own house. After a while Amaryllis suddenly announced,

'I've got to go this way,'

and headed off along a side street that, as far as he knew, was a dead end. Only of course she probably wouldn't think twice about shinning up a wall and jogging through a whole lot of back gardens. He stopped in his tracks. What if she were a spy? He had no idea at all how the intelligence services operated apart from the insight gleaned through various television programmes, both fact-based and completely fictitious. The different branches were always at war with each other and they all hated the Americans - everybody knew that - but he wasn't sure of some of the logistical aspects, such as what the retirement age was. Perhaps it was immaterial and spies always died in harness, as the horrible phrase went.

Christopher shuddered. Simon Fairfax certainly behaved like a spy, he reasoned as he continued walking, and Amaryllis had a few skills that might be useful to a spy, such as entering other people's houses illicitly, and getting into underground tunnels - not that she had been very successful at doing that, having got stuck. And were spies supposed to be afraid of spiders? Surely they were fearless, ready to go anywhere and do anything to protect the rest of us from evil... or was that Harry Potter? or Frodo Baggins?

Deep in thought, he arrived home. Big Dave had just gone out to take Marina to school - apparently she had insisted she didn't need an escort, but he had over-ruled her - and Mrs Stevenson had been left to play Monopoly with Faisal, who had his work cut out explaining the rules. He told Christopher in a stage whisper that he had already been through them twice. Well, it would keep him out of mischief. Christopher realised suddenly that Faisal should have been in school too, although under the circumstances it was only to be expected that he didn't feel up to it. He now had visions of the school attendance officer coming round with a whole regiment of social workers. He shut that out of his mind - it was the least of his worries, after all.

He rang the school anyway, and explained what had happened over the weekend, or at least the part of it that related to Faisal's mother being taken off in the ambulance. The school secretary said, 'But don't you think he would be better in school? - it would take his mind off things.'

'No,' said Christopher, who knew already how much Faisal hated school and was not about to enter into a debate about it with the school secretary in any case. Why have a long rambling pointless conversation with the monkey when you could have one later on with the organ grinder? He put the phone down. At least he had done his bit - they could worry about the rest later.

Amaryllis came down the stairs as he was still standing by the phone. She walked past him and straight into the sitting-room.

'Sorry to interrupt, guys,' she said to Mrs Stevenson and Faisal, 'only we need the parcel of money now, if you don't mind.'

Mrs Stevenson gazed at Amaryllis as if she were from another planet - which indeed could have been the case. Faisal sighed, got up and said,

'How did you know it was me?'

'Eleven-year-old boy - lots of money - Playstation games - just a wild guess,' said Amaryllis calmly.

Faisal fetched the parcel of money. He hadn't even opened it yet.

'Open it,' said Amaryllis to Christopher.

'But DNA - fingerprints - '

'It's too late for that. Just handle it yourself from here on in. I won't touch it. The police don't need to get a free sample of my DNA - it's probably on file in fifty-six countries already... Now take this - '

With a gloved hand, she gave him the envelope she had brought from her desk drawer.

'Take out one of the microdot containers - those round things. They're not the microdots themselves, you can't see those, but they hold the microdots.'

'Should I be wearing gloves?' said Christopher, trying to delay the moment when he would have to do anything difficult. He peered at the package of money, now loose and spilling out all over the coffee table. It could be radioactive as well as bugged, for all he knew.

'It's too late for that,' she repeated. 'Just open the container and scatter the dots over the money. They'll attach themselves to the raised bits on the notes. Almost impossible to detect without specialised equipment, nearly as difficult to get rid of them once they're clinging on. Great for tracking people.'

She sounded as if this was a subject very close to her heart.

'Now wrap up the parcel again,' she instructed him. He did as he was told.

Faisal watched her intently.

'Are you a spy?' he said suddenly.

Christopher did the only thing he could think of to cover up this faux pas: he had a lengthy and alarming coughing fit, causing Mrs Stevenson to pat him a bit too vigorously on the back, which in turn caused his glasses to fall off into the fireplace, from where Amaryllis retrieved them and handed them back to him with an odd look on her face. He didn't know why he had been so determined to divert everyone's attention. Perhaps he didn't really want to know whether Amaryllis was a spy or not. It was one thing for him to mull over these ideas in the privacy of his own mind, quite another for Faisal to blurt them out so that they became public property, open to the cold light of day.

He went into the kitchen for a glass of water, but as he left the living-room he heard Faisal say to Amaryllis, 'Uncle Christopher doesn't want to know if you're a spy or not....'

He deliberately didn't listen out for Amaryllis's reply.

The day's postal delivery arrived, or at least the portion of it arrived which hadn't been delivered to number forty-three, the destination for most of the mail for the street. There was an official-looking letter without logos or a sender name for Christopher. He hoped it wasn't one of these junk mailings disguised as personal letters. He particularly hated the ones from an astrologer who claimed to be able to save his life for a payment of only one thousand three hundred pounds in thirty-six convenient monthly instalments. He couldn't stand the thought that someone felt unable to make a living without conning people, and, worse still in many ways, without making up such an unconvincing back story.

It was written on headed Council paper with many intimidating phone, fax and reference numbers at the top.

'Oh, my God,' said Christopher as he read the first paragraph.

'Is it about Mum?' said Faisal, trying to sound as if he didn't really care one way or another.

'No, definitely not,' said Christopher. He looked up and gave the boy a smile that he hoped was reassuring. 'I think any news of your mum will come from the doctors once they've finished running all the tests. No, this is completely different and very annoying.'

'I didn't know Steve Paxman knew your address,' said Amaryllis, and laughed at the expression on his face. 'No, I'm not a mind reader, I just have very good eyesight. I read his name at the end.'

'It isn't from him. He's just been copied in, that's why you saw his name there. That reminds me, have you go any idea what's happened to him? I've forgotten to worry about him with all this other stuff going on.'

Amaryllis shrugged her shoulders.

'Haven't heard anything...What's the letter about then?' she said.

'This woman from the Council – Linda MacSween - wants to see our accounts,' said Christopher in a hollow voice.

'Accounts? For PLIF?'

'Exactly.'

'I've been keeping a note of what we spend,' said Mrs Stevenson suddenly. She took a small cash book out of her handbag and flipped through the pages. 'June 2nd. Meeting in Queen of Scots. Three pints of bitter, one Dubonnet and lemonade..... Seven pounds twenty.... August 4th. Meeting at the new bistro down by the harbour. Five ice-creams. Six pounds thirty-three.'

'Oh, my God,' said Christopher again, and sat down on the sofa, remembered Big Dave and Mrs Stevenson had slept on it, jumped up again and started to pace up and down the room.

Having meetings in the Queen of Scots had seemed such a reasonable thing to do – it hadn't occurred to him before that having a few drinks could be misinterpreted, or indeed that anyone was keeping track of this expenditure. After all, people couldn't be expected to turn up at meetings at all without an incentive. It was all quite harmless, and they did stick to the agenda and have minutes. Or did they?

'I thought you were meant to be the secretary?' he said to Mrs Stevenson, vaguely remembering what fun it had been choosing office-bearers in the first place, speculating on whether being chairman of PLIF absolved you from paying fines at the library for instance, or got you free bus travel, or free prescriptions, or free anything else.

'I do both,' said Mrs Stevenson grandly, turning to the back of the little book. 'PLIF steering group meeting, Queen of Scots, September tenth. Apologies from Young Dave. He had an important case going on in Stirling to do with environmental protesters. Big Dave commented that he didn't see why anyone would defend those tree-hugging porridge-weavers, especially not Young Dave whose idea of environmental protest was to complain to the landlord if the heaters weren't on in the lounge bar.'

'That's very impressive, Mrs Stevenson,' lied Christopher, becoming more horrified by the moment as the proceedings of PLIF were dragged into the limelight for the first time. He hadn't realised things were quite so well documented. This little cash book could provide valuable ammunition for Steve Paxman or the woman who had written the letter, should circumstances bring it into their hands. 'You should keep that book safe.'

'Oh, it's always safe all right,' she laughed. 'I keep a tight hold on my bag. It's got my whole life in it.'

Christopher looked at the battered old handbag and suppressed a smile.

'Oh, well,' he sighed, 'I suppose we can base some sort of accounts on your book, Mrs Stevenson. Have you ever done proper book-keeping?'

'This is how I've always done it,' said Mrs Stevenson indignantly. 'If it's good enough for Inverkeithing pensioners' Christmas Club, it's good enough for PLIF.'

'Wait a minute,' said Amaryllis. 'Why should they see your accounts? It's got nothing to do with them – you're an independent organisation, aren't you?'

'Right,' said Christopher doubtfully. After a moment he realised that in his muddle-headed state he hadn't really taken in what Amaryllis was talking about. 'What do you mean, independent?'

'I mean you're not dependent on council funding. Or at least not up to now.'

'We pay our own way,' said Mrs Stevenson indignantly. 'We all take our turn to get the drinks in – of course I can't go and stand at the bar, that wouldn't be right, but I give the money to David when it's my turn. It's nothing to do with the council.'

'I didn't mean – ,' said Amaryllis.

'No, Mrs Stevenson's right, we haven't had a penny from them,' Christopher assured her. He read the next paragraph of the letter, and felt less depressed. 'It says here the Council want to give us money.' His spirits and face fell again. 'But it's for restoring the village hall and developing a viable and socially useful programme of activities.'

'Where's the fun in that?' said Mrs Stevenson. 'Socially useful! - bleurgh.'

Amaryllis was looking very smug indeed.

'So have they actually agreed to give us the money?'

Mrs Stevenson chose to take offence. 'Some of us have been part of this for longer than others without wanting any help from the Council, and don't you forget it!'

'But have they agreed?' persisted Amaryllis.

Christopher peered at the letter again. He was having trouble taking it in - the events of the past few days had overloaded his brain, and there wasn't room for any more information in it. In his past life as an archivist he would have thought this was impossible, but then as an archivist he hadn't had much to do with real life, having spent the whole working week among historical documents. The demands of day to day living were obviously more complex than he had imagined at that time.

He read a sentence out loud to avoid having to think about it.

'The Council has money available for restoring old village halls, and if the PLIF steering group can satisfy the appropriate criteria, then an application for funding on their part for the purpose of restoring the hall at the end of Merchantman Wynd and developing socially useful community activities would have a good chance of success.'

'What are appropriate criteria?' said Faisal, just as Amaryllis asked,

'What are socially useful activities? Do they mean worthy things like knitting? Or old people's Bingo?'

'Appropriate criteria are things like having accounts, and minutes of meetings and stuff,' said Christopher to Faisal. To Amaryllis he just shrugged and smiled.

'I'd rather be in the Queen of Scots having a wee drink than hanging around some draughty hall with a lot of old people,' said Mrs Stevenson.

What do you think?' said Christopher to Amaryllis - thought he had no idea why he should trust the opinion of someone he was on the brink of deciding must be a spy.

'What do I think of what?' said Amaryllis. 'Would I rather be in the Queen of Scots or the village hall playing bingo? No contest. I'm with you, Mrs Stevenson.'

'Call me Jemima, dear,' said Mrs Stevenson.

'Why?' enquired Amaryllis, apparently as taken aback as Christopher had been at the thought that Mrs Stevenson had a first name. He decided not to tell her about Big Dave and the night on the sofa. He could hardly bear to think about it himself.

'Because it's her name,' he muttered to Amaryllis before Mrs Stevenson took serious umbrage.

'Oh, sorry Jemima,' said Amaryllis.

'No offence, dear,' said Mrs Stevenson. She winked horribly at Christopher.

'What do we have to do to get the money?' Amaryllis enquired.

'Fill in a form - you have to download it from their website, so I expect it's the kind of form that rearranges itself while you're typing into the boxes,' said Christopher darkly. He skimmed the last part of the letter. 'Funny, this woman seems to think we've already had money from them. I wonder where she got that idea.'

'That's always the question with Councils,' said Amaryllis.

'Can we call off our guerilla warfare now?' asked Christopher.

'Oh, no,' said Amaryllis, ' this is just the beginning of it.'

'Guerilla warfare?' Faisal had picked up his ears. He probably thought it was a computer game. Maybe it was. 'Guerilla Warfare for the PS3' had a certain ring of familiarity to it.

'It's a kind of war that's fought everywhere, not just on battlefields,' said Amaryllis absent-mindedly, and then, to Christopher, 'We've got to keep up the pressure now that they're softening.'

'Keep up the pressure?' said Christopher. 'We haven't even started yet - have we?'

'What do you have to do?' said Faisal.

'Well, I've started a website...' said Amaryllis.

'A guerilla warfare website! Cool!' said Faisal. 'What's the URL?'

Amaryllis wrote it down for him and he bounded off upstairs to look it up on his computer. Christopher hadn't seen his nephew bounding for quite some time; at least involving Amaryllis in their lives hadn't been all bad, he reflected.

He was still rather puzzled by this communication from the Council. What could possibly be behind it?

He must have wondered out loud, for Mrs Stevenson said wisely,

'They'll be worried about not spending their budget for the year. They get it taken away if they don't spend it, you know.'

'Is that true?' said Christopher, surprised. 'So the - ' he peered at the letterhead again, ' - the Communities and Knowledge department, which I don't believe really exists at all, incidentally, has been allocated a ridiculous amount of council taxpayers' money, and there's this pressure to spend it all on some dodgy project or other, just in case somebody realises they didn't need it in the first place and doesn't give them as much to fritter away next time.'

'Yes, that's exactly how it works,' said Mrs Stevenson, nodding and smiling. 'That's why I haven't paid any council tax for the last five years.'

'You've what?' said Christopher, aghast. He was harbouring a council tax cheat under his own roof. He had allowed her to sleep on his sofa - at this point he mentally shielded his eyes lest they inadvertently see a picture of something happening between Big Dave and - no, he mustn't go there.

'How did you get away with that?' said Amaryllis, sounding mildly interested.

Mrs Stevenson shrugged her shoulders.

'I move house a lot.'

'Does Big Dave know about this?' said Christopher sternly.

'I don't know... Big Dave isn't my keeper, you know, whatever you might think. We lead separate lives - mostly.'

Christopher tried to suppress a shudder.

'I wonder,' he said, more to divert his own attention, 'what the Communities and Knowledge department actually does.'

'Nothing, probably,' said Amaryllis, 'but at least that means they won't do as much harm as other agencies of the state bureaucracy.'

It was very strange, if Amaryllis had indeed been a spy, that she seemed to have such fervent anti-state opinions, bordering at times on -

'This may seem an odd question,' he said to her, aware that it was a complete non sequitur, 'but where do you come from?'

'Well, I live in Pitkirtly,' she said.

'But where did you come from before that? Where were you born?'

She hesitated for too long, her eyes very wary, like a wild animal who suspects there is danger round the corner. He relented and said with a smile,

'Sorry, it's none of my business. Forget it. It's got nothing to do with anything.'

Faisal came down the stairs two at a time.

'It's great!' he said to Amaryllis. 'How did you manage to get my uncle looking so - like himself?'

'Just a lucky shot,' she replied, glancing mischievously at Christopher.

'Am I on this website of yours?' said Mrs Stevenson, sitting up straight and patting her hair all round the edges of her woolly hat, which, Christopher surmised, she must have put on first thing this morning, since he didn't remember seeing her without it. He tried not to wonder if she had taken it off to go to bed, but his mind formed a hideous picture of her sitting up in bed next to Big Dave, a seemly floral flannelette nightie covering everything except her head, which wore that same hat.

'Yes, of course,' said Amaryllis. 'It wouldn't be the same without you.'

'Do you always wear that hat?' said Faisal. His uncle tried to catch his eye and signal to him to shut up, but he was staring in horrid fascination at the hat, which he had apparently just noticed.

Christopher sat down suddenly, realising that once again his knees were incapable of supporting him any longer. The weight of responsibility, which never really left him, had become unbearably heavy on his shoulders. What on earth was he going to do with the kids if Caroline never came back? In what way was he equipped to handle the village hall restoration project - it had been all right when he thought there was no way they would get the money for it - it had been a bit of harmless fun like PLIF itself, not doing anyone any harm, or indeed any good, which might have been even worse, in terms of added responsibility; now that it seemed that the Council were determined to foist the money on PLIF whether they really wanted it or not, he found it all extremely daunting.

He looked up, and found Amaryllis staring at him thoughtfully.

'I'd better ring this Linda McSween in the morning and see if I can sort out the mistake. The one about us already having funding. What was the other thing? - the parcel! What are we going to do about that?' he asked her.

At least they could get that out of the way. One less thing to worry about.

'Oh, that,' she said. 'We need to plant it back on the American.'

'How are we supposed to do that?'

'Put it in his car, deliver it through his door, I don't know....'

'But we don't know who he is or where he lives... do we?' said Christopher. Maybe this wasn't as simple as he had thought. It was even starting to sound a little dangerous.

'Can I do it?' said Faisal excitedly.

'No!' said all three adults.

'I could do it,' said Mrs Stevenson.

The idea of her being carried off to an abandoned mineshaft in the middle of nowhere had its appeal, but Christopher quickly dismissed the idea. After all, anyone who harmed her or put her in danger would have Big Dave to reckon with, and Big Dave didn't believe in making idle threats. He believed in direct action, and the sooner and more direct the better.

'Well, we've bugged it now,' said Amaryllis thoughtfully. 'If I'm going to use it to track him then I'll be tracking the person who delivers it too, so it should be quite safe.'

'It doesn't sound very safe to me,' said Christopher. He noticed all the others were looking at him with a mixture of hope and sympathy. It was a lethal combination. On the one hand he didn't want to go anywhere near the mysterious American again and on the other - well, the further away from the action he was the better. Anyway, a man with all the responsibilities he had couldn't afford to act irresponsibly, deliberately pushing himself to the brink of danger.

Just say no, urged his inner wimp, never far below the surface.

Didn't they all know he had a shift to do at the supermarket that afternoon, anyway? Which ruled him out for the rest of the day. Let them deal with it for themselves for a change.

'I'll do it tomorrow,' he said.

Chapter 13 Young Dave's crimes

'Funding?' said Christopher. 'What do you mean, funding?'

He hadn't meant to sound quite so abrupt, even when there was a woman from the Council on the other end of the line; he wished he hadn't bothered to do this before going out with the parcel of money. Being a sitting target for various villains might be preferable to dealing with the woman from the Council.

'Yes, your annual grant,' she said. There was a rustling of papers and a clicking of computer keys. 'Seven hundred and eighty-three pounds. Received on – let me see,' – click, click, rustle – 'December the fourteenth last year.'

'Annual grant?' he said faintly.

'You are Mr Wilson, aren't you? Christopher Wilson?'

He was beginning to doubt even that, but he said meekly, 'Yes, that's me.'

'Don't you remember signing the funding agreement?'

He wasn't sure what to reply to that. He certainly didn't remember, but that obviously wasn't the answer she wanted.

'Sorry,' he said at last. 'I'm going to have to look into this a bit more. Consult the rest of the steering group and so on. I'll call you back as soon as I can.'

'That's fine,' she said. 'But if there's a problem, you realise we'll have to get it sorted out before we can allocate any more funding?'

'Fine,' he agreed and rang off.

It wasn't fine at all.

He could just do without all this. Why did it have to happen now, when his life had already complicated itself beyond his wildest nightmares? It was as if, he thought gloomily and fancifully, the loom that had been programmed to weave a plain and simple fabric for his life had gone out of control, twisted the threads into ever more intricate patterns and introduced new colours which clashed horribly with the old ones.

It wasn't until he was sitting at the kitchen table with a cup of coffee that he thought of the most likely explanation for the confusion over funding: the Council had got it wrong again. They had mixed up PLIF with another, more organised organisation which had actually got itself into a position to apply for funding by having all the requisite policies, procedures, office-bearers in place and by knowing exactly which boxes to tick on which official forms and which impossible deadlines they had to meet.

On the other hand, he reasoned, if Amaryllis really wanted to pursue her vision of re-building the village hall, the confusion would have to be cleared up before PLIF could get funding for that. So he couldn't just push this whole thing to one side and ignore it for the next ten years as he would otherwise have done. It was up to him to rescue the village hall project from oblivion by forcing the Council to admit their mistake and, more important, record their admission.

This was of course the last conclusion he wanted to reach. But once he had reached it, his conscience kicked in. With a heavy heart he dialed the number for Linda McSween from the Council again, talked his way through various layers of bureaucracy and found himself speaking to her at last.

'It's Christopher Wilson. From PLIF.'

'Yes,' she said, sounding cautious.

'Are you sure about the annual grant? I mean, are you sure it was paid to PLIF? It's just that we don't seem to have a record of it…'

'There's your bank statement, surely,' she pointed out.

'Bank statement? But – '

'It was definitely paid to a bank account in the name of the Pitkirtly Local Improvement Forum,' she said firmly. 'That's what PLIF stands for, isn't it?'

'But why - ? I mean, did we apply for it?'

'You are the chairman, aren't you, Mr Wilson?'

'Yes, but – '

'In that case you're the person ultimately responsible for the funding application – even if you delegated that responsibility to somebody else.'

'Delegated?'

Christopher told himself to try not to sound like such a complete idiot. It was hard not to, when he felt like one.

'Maybe somebody else filled in the form for you,' she explained patiently. There was a rustling again. 'But you do seem to have signed it, Mr Wilson. You and a Mr Jackson.'

'Mr Jackson?'

'Mr Jackson, your treasurer.'

'Treasurer? But – I mean, I see. Sorry to have bothered you.'

'No problem.'

She seemed to have a smile in her voice this time as she rang off. He was sure his phone call would provide plenty of harmless amusement at the West Fife

Communities and Knowledge Department. Goodness knows they must need it in their line of work.

Mr Jackson was Young Dave. But it was news to Christopher that he was treasurer of PLIF, unless Mrs Stevenson had delegated this responsibility to him since he last spoke to her. Could somebody have forged both his and Christopher's signatures on the form, set up a bank account in the name of PLIF and walked off with the princely sum of seven hundred and eighty three pounds? And would it be worth anybody's while to do that?

With an even heavier heart Christopher realised he would have to speak to Young Dave as soon as possible. He feared Young Dave would go on the defensive right away – which of course was his default position in most situations – and once that happened they wouldn't be able to have a proper conversation.

After he had finally decided this could wait until later, and in fact wouldn't Young Dave be at work at this time on a Tuesday, the phone rang almost under his hand. He couldn't remember dealing with so many phone calls in such a short time since his father had died and he had to ring round assorted relatives to break the news. At least this time nobody had died, he told himself, shutting out the voice in his head that added 'yet' to the sentence.

'Why, Christopher!' said Maisie Sue – or was it Susie Mae? He still hadn't got the name fixed in his head. 'You sure have been a busy bee this morning! I've been trying to reach you for an hour.'

'Hello,' he said.

'It's Maisie Sue McPherson? I wonder if you have a minute to talk?'

Yes, I wonder that too, thought Christopher; even a minute to stand irresolutely without talking or even thinking would be nice. Instead of putting this into words he said, 'Yes, of course, Maisie Sue. But only a minute – I have something urgent to do – um, somewhere – after that.'

'I've had an idea?' she said. 'It may sound wacky or way-out to you, but once I had it, I said to myself, I must call Christopher about this! Pearson said no, leave the man alone, he doesn't want to be bothered with it, but I – '

'Pearson?' he interrupted, unwilling to engage with the woman but unable to suppress his curiosity.

'Pearson – that's my husband? I can't believe I didn't mention him to you already!'

She said something else in an undertone, and he heard her laughter and perhaps someone else's in the background.

'Pearson can't believe it either?'

'I'm sure he can't.'

'Anyways – where was I? Oh, yes, I've had an idea? If you don't want to take up my previous idea of barn-raising, maybe you'll like this one better. Are you listening?'

'Yes.'

'How about we all get together and hold a yard sale?'

'A yard sale?'

'Oh, sorry, you don't use that term for it. Pearson says to tell you it's a kind of Christmas fair? To get money for the village hall? I and my little group think it would be really neat if we had some place like that to meet, and we'd like to help.'

'A Christmas Fair. Hmm.'

'You don't like it!'

'No, it isn't that at all,' Christopher lied through his teeth. He hated the idea; he was sure a Christmas Fair would have all the ingredients of one of his worst nightmares. Still, Christmas was quite a way off. A lot of water would have flowed down the Kirtly burn by then. Maybe it wouldn't do any harm to agree to the suggestion for now, and review it later, deciding reluctantly that it wouldn't work, for some reason that didn't immediately spring to mind but that he felt he could rely on Jock McLean to dream up. 'I think it's a great idea,' he added.

'Oooh!' A girlish scream hit the ear he was holding the phone to, and he quickly transferred it to the other ear to give the first one a chance to recover. 'I'm so sorry, Christopher,' she added at a lower level of decibels. 'I got carried away by the excitement? We'll start organising right now! I can't wait to tell the girls.'

'Good,' he said. It sounded hollow to him but maybe Maisie Sue didn't notice.

Chapter 14   Desperately seeking…

Now that he at last had time to find one of the mysterious strangers who had been complicating his life for the past week, of course there was no sign of any of them. After following Christopher around relentlessly for days, they must all have decided to have a break from it. Or perhaps one of them was just sitting back monitoring Christopher's whereabouts electronically using the bugs planted in the parcel of money instead of having to use a shiny black or other appropriate car. More environmentally friendly, after all. And cheaper for whoever his paymasters were. Christopher no longer thought one of the paymasters was Her Majesty's Revenue and Customs. It was obviously something far more sinister. The CIA, perhaps, or a similarly ruthless organisation. And was there still a KGB?

It was funny that before Christopher had ever encountered Simon Fairfax, he had found Steve Paxman a bit sinister. Now the latter seemed more like a powerless puppet, tied up so tightly in red tape himself that he wouldn't have been able to get a hand free to tie anyone else up in it even if that had been his mission. Christopher even felt the tiniest crumb of compassion for the man. He had probably led a completely grey colourless life too. Monochrome man, that was Steve. The most exciting thing he had ever done was to disappear suddenly and without a trace.

Simon, on the other hand, had probably been round the world several times, leaving a trail of people terminated with extreme prejudice, and perhaps a selection of heartbroken women too. Maybe Amaryllis had been one of them, and that was why she was so determined to work against him. Christopher's intellect told him that Simon and Amaryllis could still be working together, but the softer part of his brain - he refused to think of it as his heart - said they weren't. He didn't want to explore the reasoning behind that for the moment. There would come a time when it was right to do so.

Christopher's mobile phone rang. He contemplated switching it off again, but Amaryllis, Faisal, Mrs Stevenson and Big Dave, who had returned traumatised after his trip to the school gates with Marina, had all insisted that he switched it on and left it on, in case of emergency. Big Dave had been very indignant about the language he had heard in the playground. 'I've never heard anything like it! All that swearing, and the grammar! It's not a very good example for the teachers to set!' Nobody could work out whether he was joking or not.

'Hello,' said Christopher cautiously, hoping he was speaking into the right part of the phone.

'Egglegig.... Memorial....'

'Egglegig?'

'I'm sorry,' said the voice at the other end, more clearly now. 'Did you say Egglegig?'

'Yes but - who is this?'

'Is that Mr Wilson?'

'Yes,' he said even more cautiously.

'It's Estelle McCrone, the nursing supervisor at Kirkcaldy Memorial Hospital, Mr Wilson. I've got bad news, I'm afraid.'

'Caroline? She's not - has something gone wrong?'

'Something has indeed gone wrong,' said the nursing supervisor severely. 'I'm afraid your sister has walked out of the hospital - wearing a hospital gown, which will of course need to be returned in good condition to us as soon as possible - and still in a confused state and in need of medical attention.'

'Walked out? You mean she's escaped?'

'She hasn't escaped, Mr Wilson, this isn't a prison, you know,' said the nursing supervisor reprovingly. 'But we are concerned for her health and safety, and yes, she is missing.'

'Missing? You've lost her?'

'I must emphasise that she left apparently of her own volition, Mr Wilson.'

There was a pause, during which Christopher quickly evaluated various possible responses. His initial thought was to reply 'What do you expect me to do about it?' but he didn't want to invite further censure from the nursing supervisor.

'So - have you sent somebody out looking for her then?' he said hopefully.

There was an indrawn breath from the other end of the phone - or perhaps just a burst of static.

'My nursing staff can't spend their time out looking for an adult who decides of their own free will to discharge themselves in an unconventional manner,' said the nursing supervisor frostily. 'But,' she added, softening slightly, 'I've reported the incident to the police, and they will no doubt be in touch with you in due course.'

'The police?'

The last thing Christopher needed at this point was for the police to get in touch with him for the third time in as many days. But he hoped if the police were out looking for Caroline then he wouldn't have to be involved.

'Yes, indeed. Under the circumstances that seems to be appropriate.'

'Thanks for letting me know,' he said, feeling foolish.

'Goodbye, Mr Wilson.'

No sooner had she rung off that the phone rang again. Christopher hadn't had this many mobile phone calls since Marina had been in trouble at school and Caroline had given them his number so that she wouldn't have to interrupt her daytime television viewing to answer the phone.

'It's Mrs Wingford,' said a brisk voice. Surely it couldn't be another nursing supervisor. It did sound very much like one, though.

'Head teacher at Pitkirtly High School,' she added helpfully. 'Is that Mr Wilson?'

'Yes,' he said reluctantly. She would track him down eventually, even if he put her off now.

'I just wanted to alert you to the fact that Marina was seen talking to a very odd-looking man outside the school this morning, and we thought you should be aware - '

'What sort of man?' said Christopher, feeling somewhat at a loss. Again, what did they expect him to do about it? After all, it wasn't as if Marina had gone to school on her own; she had been escorted by Big Dave, who surely would have -

'Was he big and - well, big, with dark hair and a beard, and wearing a woolly hat?' he said, interrupting Mrs Wingford's ramblings.

'As I was saying,' said Mrs Wingford reprovingly, perhaps on the verge of telling him off for interrupting, 'I have a note here of what he looked like. Yes, big, dark hair, beard, woolly hat - seemed scruffy - shoes worn down at the heel slightly - possibly a rough sleeper - query alcohol problems...'

'With all due respect, Mrs Wingford,' said Christopher, offended on Big Dave's behalf by this woman who thought she could diagnose alcohol problems by looking at someone's shoes, 'I don't see how you can diagnose alcoholism by looking at someone's shoes. If you could, then maybe my sister would have got treatment years ago instead of having to wait until a crisis developed. The man you're describing is a close personal friend of mine and I don't think he would be very pleased if he could hear you describing him in this way.'

Christopher felt weak at the knees by the time he had finished this little speech.

'Sorry, Mr Wilson, I couldn't hear all of that,' said Mrs Wingford. 'We get a lot of static in school from the overhead pylons.'

'The man's a friend of mine!' shouted Christopher into the phone. 'There's no need to worry!'

'Well, if you're sure,' said Mrs Wingford, still with that note of disapproval in her voice. 'It was just that nobody had seen him around the school gates before, and one of our mothers thought - '

'No, it's fine,' said Christopher. 'But thank you for your vigilance.'

'You can't be too careful, Mr Wilson,' said Mrs Wingford, and ended the call.

Christopher was of the opinion that you could be too careful, but he didn't have the time or energy to develop an argument about it at this moment. He wondered about calling the police to ask about if they had started to search for Caroline, but he didn't know where he should ring. Big Dave had told him all calls went through a call centre in Stirling, but he didn't really believe that. Surely they must have someone closer by who answered the phone. In any case he didn't know what number to dial: it probably didn't count as a 999 situation, as far as he knew anyway. They would have to contact him if they wanted him. He must force himself to concentrate on finding the right person to give the parcel to.

He realised that his feet, as if they were propelled by his sub-conscious, which had obviously been working away underneath while his conscious mind dealt with Mrs Wingford, were taking him down the road that led to the harbour. It made a certain amount of sense to look for the mysterious strangers there, since it was one of Simon's known haunts as well as quite near where the shooting incident had taken place.

Christopher had just arrived at the harbour wall, though without sighting any mysterious strangers or their cars, when the phone rang again. Silently cursing the invention of mobile technology, which could interrupt and disrupt your life on a whim because people were nowadays too impatient to use the less intrusive methods which were still at their disposal, he answered it.

'It's Sergeant McLuskey from Leven Road police station, Kirkcaldy,' said a male voice, less peremptory than that of the two women who had earlier rung him in rapid succession; instead there was a note of world-weariness, as if its owner had seen all the foibles and failings of people and, although despairing of making a difference, would keep on trying because it was his job to do so. Christopher marvelled himself for discerning so much from one sentence. Something of Mrs Wingford's psychological insight must have rubbed off on him.

'Is there any news of Caroline - Mrs Hussein?' asked Christopher.

'We've located your sister, Mr Wilson. But she's refusing to come down as yet. We've sent for an expert to try and talk her down safely, but it's going to take him a while to get here from North Berwick.'

'Talk her down?'

'I'm afraid your sister has managed to get up on the hospital roof and she's threatening to jump.'

Christopher tried to picture how tall the hospital building was, and how far Caroline might fall, and failed. He couldn't remember much about it at all. But even if it wasn't any bigger than a house, she could still injure herself - or worse. This was dreadful. He must keep calm.

'Isn't there any other way of getting her down? A turntable ladder? A helicopter?'

'She could easily jump while we're putting something in place. We're trying our best, Mr Wilson. But we feel it might be useful for someone from her family to have a word with her.'

'Me?'

It came out as an affronted squeak.

'I understand there are children....' said Sergeant McLuskey, doubtfully.

'No - no - they're too young,' said Christopher. 'I couldn't possibly put them through that. No, I'd better come over. It'll take me a while - the buses.....'

'We'll send a car round for you,' said Sergeant McLuskey. 'Where are you? Anywhere near home?'

'Well, I'm in Pitkirtly, but down by the harbour.'

'Stay where you are. They'll pick you up there.'

'But - '

Christopher wanted to tell the sergeant he was on an important errand, but as soon as he started to think about framing a sentence, it became impossible to explain. He sat on the harbour wall, clutching the parcel and shivering a little in the cold damp October air, and rang home. It was

178

engaged. He tried again. Still engaged. He told himself to wait a bit, trying to curb the sense of panic that was threatening to engulf him. What was happening at home? Who was on the phone and why? Did they need him there, or were they wondering where he was and what was happening?

A police car came hurtling down the road, sirens blaring, lights flashing, and screeched to a halt.

'Mr Christopher Wilson?' said the driver.

'Yes, that's me,' said Christopher, getting into the car.

It was flashing lights and blaring sirens, and swinging round corners, and overtaking on the inside on the dual carriageway, and eyes tightly shut, all the way to Kirkcaldy, but suddenly everything went quiet and the car was creeping up the hospital drive, adhering closely to the 5 mph speed limit. An idiot in a 4 x 4 who had turned into the hospital grounds just behind the police car started beeping his horn at them.

'Don't want to advertise ourselves,' said the driver. 'We might scare her into doing something silly.'

Well, thought Christopher, how much sillier can she get? Jumping off the hospital roof wouldn't stand out in her life as a particularly silly thing to do but as the logical consequence of her actions to date.

The 4 x 4 turned off into the car park, and the police car crept closer to the hospital building.

Suddenly Christopher saw a little cluster of people standing looking up at the roof.

'I've got to get out,' he said urgently.

'We're taking you round to the back, sir,' said the police officer who had been sitting quietly next to the driver, as still as an Action Man, which he quite closely resembled, especially since he had apparently not even batted an eyelid at any of the corners they had come round on two wheels on the way here. 'There's a way up on to the roof.'

'On to the roof? Me?'

'That's the general idea, sir,' said the policeman with a sideways look at his colleague, the driver.

'Isn't that a bit - '

He stopped in mid-sentence. The missing word was 'dangerous'. He didn't really want to ask baldly what if Caroline decided to push him off the roof, but couldn't work out how to phrase it so that he didn't seem like a terrible wimp.

'We won't be very far away.' The driver obviously meant to sound reassuring, but the effect of his words was to paint a picture in Christopher's mind of himself and Caroline wrestling at the very edge of the roof, and the police arriving just too late to save him from falling. Or maybe they would fall together like a pair of lovers who had decided to jump together. And what would happen to Faisal and Marina then?

He gasped for air. Somewhere in the distance he heard sirens – or maybe they were in his imagination. He hoped they heralded the arrival of a fire engine with a big ladder.

Halfway up the back stairs he realised he was still clutching the parcel with which they had hoped to trap one of the mysterious strangers. Oh, well, too late to worry about that now. Simon Fairfax and Amaryllis Peebles would just have to work things out with the American and all the rest themselves, without trying to involve innocent bystanders in it. He hung on to the parcel anyway. There was nowhere else to put it.

He tripped on the stairs just thinking about all of this; paused to say to himself, what chance have I got on the roof if I can't manage the stairs? He told himself sternly to lay off the negative self-talk; tripped again while pondering this.

'Mind your step there, sir,' said one of the police officers. He hoped they weren't laughing at him, or at least not unduly.

The stairs seemed endless and yet it was much too soon when they arrived at the door that led to the roof. It seemed ludicrously easy to get out there - surely they must have lost patients like this before?

'I suppose this door's usually locked,' he commented. The nearest policeman just shrugged his shoulders and rolled his eyes at the same time. Christopher was impressed by his co-ordination.

'So anybody can just get out on the roof any time?' he persisted.

'I believe it's used routinely by staff who want to contravene the smoking regulations,' said the other policeman, the one who had been driving.

Indeed, there was a smell of cigarettes as they came out into the open air. They were met by another police officer who introduced himself as Sergeant McLuskey.

'You made good time,' he whispered. 'We weren't expecting you for another ten minutes yet.'

'We just put the sirens on and went for it,' said the policeman who hadn't been driving, modestly.

'So - are you ready for this?' said Sergeant McLuskey to Christopher.

'I don't think so,' said Christopher. 'What should I say to her? How near should I get?'

'Don't rush in too close, Mr Wilson. You could shock her into jumping. We'll give you a loud-hailer and you can stand well back... Just tell her who you are for starters.'

Christopher sincerely hoped Caroline wouldn't jump as soon as she heard his voice. It would be a bit embarrassing. No, that was the wrong word for it.

He didn't have time to think of the right word. Sergeant McLuskey took him by the arm and led - or possibly dragged - him forward. The policeman himself picked up the loud-hailer and spoke into it first.

'Mrs Hussein! Caroline!' he said.

His magnified and distorted voice echoed round the roof. Christopher could now see the lonely little figure standing much too near the edge, at the front of the roof. She half-turned and looked at them.

'Caroline, I've got your brother here. He wants to speak to you.'

'Christopher?' said Caroline in mild surprise. Her voice was a bit indistinct. Christopher hoped there wouldn't be any silly misunderstandings, each not really catching what the other said, that would lead to disaster. It would be one thing to jump because you were in despair and your life was a mess - he could almost sympathise with that under the circumstances - but another altogether to jump because you thought someone had told you there were twenty firemen below ready to catch you when there weren't.

'If you keep her talking long enough, we might be able to get the big ladder up,' murmured Sergeant McLuskey.

There was just a spit of rain in the air. Christopher gingerly took the loud-hailer which the other man held out to him. He transferred the parcel of money to his spare hand.

'Caroline!' he called.

Sergeant McLuskey winced. 'You don't need to shout, sir. They'll probably have heard that in Dundee.'

'Caroline, it's Christopher here. Can you come here and talk to me? Maybe we can just have a quiet word.... It's a bit more sheltered over here.'

'What's the point?' she shouted. 'We've had plenty of time to talk over the last forty-three years. It's all been such a waste.'

'Maybe I wasn't listening before,' said Christopher.

'No use... nobody listening now?'

She half-turned away from him; some of her words were caught on the wind and whisked away over the edge of the roof. He knew he must try to get her to look at him properly.

'I've got plenty of time to listen,' he said. 'I want to know what – what you want.'

'What I want – what you want – what I want.' She took a step nearer the edge. Christopher started forward. Sergeant McLuskey muttered 'No!... Say something about the family – your childhood.'

Christopher trawled his memory for anything resembling lost treasure.

'Remember when we found that dead fox in the garden?' he shouted. 'The one we hid in the compost heap?'

She seemed to be hovering right on the edge.

'Remember that Christmas when I hid your presents and you thought Santa had forgotten you?'

'Christmas!' she moaned, swaying a little.

183

'There was the time Mr Browning ran over your bike...'

Christopher realised the only memories he could dredge up were depressing ones.

Sergeant McLuskey sighed heavily. 'The children?' he suggested.

'What about Marina? And Faisal? They're not a waste. They just want you home. They're really missing you.' Christopher wasn't sure if it was a good idea to mention the kids, let alone lie about how they felt. Maybe her despair was caused partly by her failure to look after them properly. He saw her shoulders slump. He felt panic tightening his chest and starting to choke him. Surely he wasn't going to have a heart attack, on top of everything else? That would be very annoying.

She turned away from the edge and started to walk towards them.

'I can't do it,' she was saying to herself. 'I can't leave them yet after all.'

She stumbled as she came nearer, and Christopher went forward to help her up. She leaned against him heavily, so that he staggered back. Sergeant McLuskey, treading carefully as if on eggshells, came forward to help him. Caroline didn't even notice him. Christopher put his arms round her, not really wanting to but feeling he had to.

'What's all this about, Caroline?' he said to her, while knowing he wouldn't understand even if she were capable of explaining it to him.

'I can't do it any more,' she sobbed. 'The kids - the teachers looking at me - the social workers...'

'The social workers?' he said. 'What do you mean, social workers?'

'Try not to upset her,' whispered Sergeant McLuskey into his ear. 'We've got to get her downstairs.'

'Social workers coming to the house....I can't do it.'

There were people in white coats and others in hospital scrubs, some with flapping white hats, coming up the stairs to meet them. Christopher surrendered her to them, and they hurried her away, he hoped towards a sleep and a forgetting, or other appropriate quotation for drug-induced unconsciousness. There would be time later to work out what was behind it all. He wouldn't be altogether surprised to find she had conjured up the social workers from her imagination. But it seemed an odd kind of monster to think up - why not werewolves, or zombies, or evil fantasy creatures from some made-for-television movie? If you were going to use your imagination you might as well use it for something worthwhile.

He, Sergeant McLuskey and the two other policemen walked back down the stairs. Christopher was just wondering if there was another way to get home that didn't involve closed eyes and white knuckles, when there was a commotion not far away.

'Get your hands off me, you - you terrorists!' screeched Caroline's voice. 'I've got to go with my brother! He's in danger!'

Running footsteps, shouting, wild random screeching from Caroline. Then she appeared on the stairs below them.

'Christopher! I've got to come with you....I promised my mother on her death-bed.... Keep back, you - you vandals!'

'It's all right, Caroline, they're just trying to help you,' said Christopher, although he was touched by her apparent need to protect him from imagined danger.

She stared up at him, wide-eyed.

'Come on, you can get rid of those policemen, and come with me!'

Someone crept up behind her; she wavered, her eyelids flickered, she fell into the arms of one of the medical team, eyes closed, at peace - although Christopher was reminded of the 'to be or not to be' speech from 'Hamlet' - ' in that sleep of death what dreams may come?' None of them knew what sort of dreams they were forcing her into. Perhaps that was where the social workers had come from.

'You OK, Mr Wilson?' said Sergeant McLuskey, looking at him with concern. 'That was quite an outburst, wasn't it?'

'I'm used to Caroline,' said Christopher ruefully.

'How about a cup of tea in the canteen before the boys drive you home,' suggested the Sergeant. 'Unless you want to go and see your sister settled down.'

'No, not really,' said Christopher. 'I'd like a breath of fresh air, and some time on my own, if you don't mind.'

'That's fine, Mr Wilson. I'll have the car standing by. Just give me a shout when you're ready.'

Christopher barely managed to thank them for their help before stumbling helplessly down the rest of the staircase and out the door at the bottom, eyes blurred and watery, hands shaking so much he was afraid he was going to drop the parcel. He didn't really know why he was hanging on to it; it was only money, when all was said and done. It didn't live, and breathe, and drink and swear, and play Monopoly, and get stuck behind sinks in old village halls... Ever since that day when Amaryllis had first appeared in the Queen of Scots, his life and all his thoughts seemed to have been turned upside down and shaken about, almost as if he had been living inside a tornado for a week or so.

'Hello, Mr Wilson,' said a familiar voice as he emerged into the open. 'I thought I might find you here.'

The sleek black car was parked, audaciously, next to the police car Christopher had arrived in. Simon Fairfax was standing by the driver's door and a dark-skinned heavy-set man was glowering from the front passenger seat. Christopher's search for mysterious strangers was over.

Chapter 15 The road to Auchterderran

Simon Fairfax's friend or colleague was a big hairy man whom it would have been grossly insulting to gorillas to compare with a gorilla. He and Simon between them bundled Christopher quickly and efficiently into the sleek black car. There was no chance to call for help, to try and run back into the building, or to attract attention in any way whatsoever. There was no sign of the policemen who had been all over the place only minutes before. It was the stuff of Christopher's nightmares.

Simon's accomplice drove off down the hospital drive somewhat more speedily than Christopher had driven up it in the police car, but after that he settled down to a steady pace which presumably he thought would not attract anyone's attention.

'Where are we going?' said Christopher.

'Where do you want to go?' said Simon Fairfax, beside him in the back seat while the big hairy man drove. Simon gave a false and chilling smile, flashing his teeth as, Christopher imagined, a crocodile might have done under similar circumstances.

'Home,' said Christopher.

'I don't think that's an option at the moment - is it, Feroze?' said Simon cheerfully. 'We were thinking more in terms of a friendly drive up to an old mineshaft we know near Auchterderran, and then a friendly conversation, and then after that we would take you home. Providing the conversation goes as we would like it go, that is. Right, Feroze?'

'Right, Mr Fairfax,' said Feroze, giving a grin over his shoulder that was if anything slightly more unnerving than Simon's smile. He had a kind of quasi-American accent which Christopher thought he might have acquired by watching too many gangster movies.

'Feroze isn't very happy right now,' said Simon. He glanced sideways at Christopher. 'Aren't you going to ask me why?'

'Why?' said Christopher, not really wanting to know.

'His friend got shot in the street when he was just trying to attract your attention. The American killed him. But you've led a charmed life until now, haven't you?'

'Nothing to do with me,' said Christopher. 'I'm just an innocent bystander in all this.'

'There's no such thing,' said Simon.

'You're not with Her Majesty's Revenue and Customs at all, are you?' said Christopher. He wasn't sure if he should be saying anything, but his nerves were too jangled to let him sit in stony silence while they drove him towards his doom.

'Not at this precise moment, no,' said Simon, his smile broadening. 'I do sometimes feel as if I worked for them, the amount of tax I have to pay. But I'm not officially employed by them, no.'

'Have you ever been?' said Christopher rashly.

'Not as such,' said Simon.

There was a silence.

'Do you mind if I just call home on my mobile?' said Christopher politely. 'They might be worrying about me - they didn't know I was going to have to come to the hospital.'

'Better not,' said Simon. 'Let's see your mobile - I have an interest in technological developments.'

Christopher fumbled around in his jacket pocket, not really intending to hand over his mobile but feeling to see if he had anything useful on him, such as a flick-knife, a small pistol or even a plastic fork to jam in Simon's eye.

'I don't have it,' he lied.

'Oh, dear, Christopher, some are born to lie and others have lying thrust upon them and don't do it very convincingly,' said Simon. He delved into the pocket, extracted the mobile, glanced at it scornfully, then wound down the window and threw it out.

'That was a bit silly,' said Christopher mildly. He wasn't sure how to react to any of it. Nothing in his life to date had prepared him for this. Amaryllis would have been much better at dealing with the situation.

'Whatever,' said Simon. He leaned over the driver's shoulder to give him directions in a low voice. They had driven through Kirkcaldy and out the other side and turned down a minor road that was signposted for Glenrothes, not the most attractive destination at the best of times and now its name sounded even grimmer and more portentous than usual. The hairy man was driving a little too fast for the narrow road, but, reasoned Christopher, if they had an accident he was more likely to get the chance to escape, as Harrison Ford had done in 'The Fugitive'.

The rain that had been spitting on Christopher earlier when he was on the hospital roof was now heavier and more unpleasant. There were potholes at the sides of the road, filling rapidly with water.

'It'll be a bit bleak on the moors in this,' said Simon. He glanced at Christopher's waterproof parka. 'Just as well you wrapped up warm.'

For the first time in his life, Christopher actually envied his sister Caroline. Not for her the panic and the fear and the visions of the abandoned mineshaft. She would still be unconscious, tucked up in bed with people watching over her. He wondered what she had meant by insisting he was in danger. As it had turned out, she was right - but it must have just been a fluke that she had said it. Surely she had nothing to do with - Surely she and her fugitive Iranian husband - Surely the fugitive Iranian husband with all the contacts in various underworlds.....

It was as if a great light had been switched on in his mind, but it illuminated something horrible which would have been better to remain in darkness. Christopher didn't want to say any more or think any more. He would wait for the 'conversation' at the top of the abandoned mineshaft. There was always the chance that these two would be so keen to boast about what they had done that they would just carry on talking while he himself faded away into the background, disappearing into the landscape as the Picts were once thought to have done.

'Damn,' said Simon Fairfax suddenly, as they drove through a small village with a very long main street, a sign that it had once been a mining town. 'We've gone the wrong way.'

A glimmer of hope. As soon as bad people started to make mistakes, they were fatally weakened, because it no longer seemed that things would go exactly according to plan for them, and if one thing had gone wrong, then other things could too.

'Easy,' said the hairy man at the wheel, swinging round and driving down an even smaller side road. 'If we head up to Kinglassie now we can get back on track. We'll be coming at the moor from the opposite direction, is all.'

It was hard to tell what his accent was. It alternated between the pseudo-American drawl and some sort of

Middle Eastern cadences. It didn't matter anyway, and Christopher knew he was only worrying about Feroze's accent to keep his mind off other more unpleasant things such as Iranian gangsters and their ways.

The others, back at the house, had no idea of what was going on or where he was. Christopher realised he hadn't even called them to let them know about Caroline and the roof - partly because he hadn't wanted to worry Faisal. Now he wished he had at least given them a clue about his whereabouts. At least they could have tracked him as far as the hospital, and someone might have seen him leaving there - although that was a faint hope since most of the spectators had probably gathered round at the front of the building at least for as long as there was the chance of drama and bloodshed. He shivered. Maybe the police would notice he was missing, but they would probably just think he had either gone off to the station, caught a bus or got a lift from someone he knew, and would have dismissed him as ungrateful and rude for disappearing without letting them know he didn't want a ride home in a police car. All the ways he imagined being rescued were closing down, one by one.

They went through Kinglassie. If only they had stopped, even at a pedestrian crossing, Christopher thought he might have been able to attract attention, or even jump out. He tried to wind down his window surreptitiously. It was jammed. Simon Fairfax smiled unpleasantly again.

'The wonders of technology, Christopher.'

The use of his first name by someone who only meant him harm was really starting to bug him, Christopher thought, although then again it would have been ridiculous for Simon to call him 'Mr Wilson' at this

192

point. He started to think about whether the kids would miss him or not, but he had to stop his thoughts from going down that route as it was too upsetting, and he didn't want to be a sentimental wreck when they got out of the car, as he was sure they would, on a deserted moor or hillside near Auchterderran village. He wondered if Caroline would ever recover. He wasn't sure exactly what was wrong with her but it must be connected with her alcoholism. Alcoholic dementia? Delirium tremens? He didn't know enough about the medical stuff to work it out himself. That was what doctors were for - not that they had shown any sign of working it out up to now. Now that they had her in their hands it must get a little easier, surely, if only they could keep her in their hands for long enough - what if she went up on the roof again, and he wasn't around to be called in? Marina and Faisal might have to go through the whole crisis with her. All his thoughts led back to them.

It was too difficult thinking all these thoughts, so he looked mindlessly out of the car window for a while, not even really seeing the scenery as it changed from long mining village to scrubby moorland and back.

The car slowed, the dark hairy man drove it up a track that led into the moor, it stopped.

'Let's get out and walk for a bit,' said Simon easily, as if he was suggesting a Sunday afternoon stroll. They all got out of the car. Christopher was still clutching the parcel, under his arm now. Nobody seemed to notice it. Perhaps even at this late stage he could use the money to bribe Simon Fairfax.

They left the track and wandered across moorland. There were few trees, and the ones that had managed to get a hold were stunted and bare of leaves, poisoned by industry that had swept through this area like a whirlwind and then had gone again almost overnight, leaving a trail of destruction behind it. If he made a run for it, which in itself was unlikely since he didn't trust his running prowess to get him away from pursuers, there would be nowhere to hide, and no-one to help him. It would have been easy to collapse in despair, falling to his knees and whimpering, but Christopher was incapable of that kind of loss of self-control. He wondered how far it would be to the abandoned mineshaft, the sudden push and then either the quick death caused by the fall or the slow lingering death in the lonely darkness at the bottom of the pit.

'This way,' said Simon, as if ushering him to a seat in a restaurant or the theatre. He led the small party as if he knew exactly where he was going. Had he done this before? Would Christopher join a pitiful heap of other human remains when he fell?

'I don't know why you're doing this, but have you thought that you might have the wrong person?' suggested Christopher, knowing he had to delay things somehow.

'I don't think so. Christopher Wilson, redundant archivist, the brother of Caroline Hussein, whom he has been harbouring in his home for a time along with her children Marina and Faisal,' said Simon, reeling it all off as if he had rehearsed for this very moment.

'But why?' said Christopher.

Simon smiled again, grimly. 'If you're expecting this to turn into one of those murder stories where the villain can't resist telling everything before he kills someone, and then the rescuers arrive over the horizon, you're very much mistaken,' he said. 'The deal is, we all keep quiet and do this with no fuss.'

'That may be your idea of a deal,' said Christopher, stopping and turning to face Simon. 'It isn't anything I've agreed to.'

'Christopher, you're so perfect!' said Simon, laughing out loud this time. 'You don't agree to being abducted and murdered - that isn't how it works! Has nobody ever told you?'

'I don't mix in that kind of circle,' said Christopher stiffly. Over Simon's shoulder he found he could see the place where Feroze had parked the car. And - his heart jumped - there was another car parked next to it. He didn't want to stare for too long in case Simon noticed something, so he couldn't tell much about the other car, except that it wasn't a police car or at least not a marked one. The only thing he sure of was that he wasn't hallucinating. Just when he had thought he was on his own with nobody to turn to, there was somebody else there! He glanced around wildly.

'No, there's nobody to turn to,' said Simon coldly. 'Nowhere to go. Come on, let's get this over with.'

He gestured to his dark hairy accomplice, who now took Christopher by the shoulder, threatening to dislodge the parcel from under his arm, and pulled him on forward. At the last moment Christopher managed to transfer the parcel to his other side. It was like being trapped in a giant industrial clamp.

They must have walked just over half a mile from the road, which was now hidden from view by the series of lumps and bumps in the ground which were probably man-made but which had become absorbed into the landscape, producing an odd effect. It was similar to what Christopher imagined the surface of the moon would look like, except for being green rather than whatever colour the moon surface was, he thought brownish. His thoughts were now rambling, an uncharacteristic sensation. Was this similar to the feeling of your whole life flashing before you when you were drowning? It didn't seem so, since Christopher's life to date had been controlled, organised, categorised to the point of boredom, whereas his thoughts now were dotting about all over the place and dredging up little snippets of half-remembered information randomly from his own personal archives.

They were out of sight of the place where the cars were parked too, and there had been no sign of anyone else about.

No, wait! A figure came into view on the top of one of the bumps in the ground.

Christopher waved frantically with the hand that wasn't rendered numb by Feroze's grasp on his shoulder. It was the hand that now held the parcel, but he was less bothered about that than about attracting someone's attention, even if they were an innocent passer-by who didn't deserve to be dragged into this situation.

After a minute the figure waved its hand back. There was no sign of urgency, of phoning the police on a mobile, of running to flag down a car on the road and get help. Christopher lowered his hand, deflated. But surely this person would notice something was wrong if Christopher suddenly disappeared, or if three men walked off across the moor and only two returned. He was a witness, if nothing else.

'Nice try,' said Simon. 'There's no help for you there.'

'He could get you into trouble, though,' said Christopher. 'He'll remember us.'

'I don't think so,' said Simon, smirking now. He seemed to have a range of smiles for every occasion, each more unpleasant than the previous.

'But how can you be sure?' persisted Christopher. He was rapidly reaching the stage of not caring what he said.

'Because, Christopher, he's one of ours. He's been following us on his motorbike ever since we left the hospital... Sorry,' Simon added after a slight pause during which Christopher's spirits plummeted and his face felt as if it had done the same. 'He'll only remember what we tell him to remember. Two men setting out across the moor for a bracing health-giving walk such as the government are always trying to persuade us to do, and two men coming back to their car.'

'We're about there,' said Feroze suddenly. 'Watch your step.'

Christopher looked all around him, memorising the wet feel of the rain as it spattered his face, the sponginess of the turf under his feet, the grey cloudy skies that always looked so big when you were outside town, the greenness of the grass.... He couldn't even imagine not being able to feel or see any of it again. He couldn't imagine how his family would cope without him. And as an afterthought, he allowed himself to think about Amaryllis, cool and yet somehow vulnerable, her child-like delight in playing Monopoly and her plotting and planning, the panic she must have felt being trapped with spiders. The view from her balcony.

How unfair to lose all this before it had really begun. He blinked back raindrops mingled with self-pitying tears.

'Turn around,' said Simon. Not a trace of a smile now.

Christopher turned around, assisted by Feroze's grip on his shoulder which forced him to face Simon. Then Feroze let him go for a moment while he took off a backpack and started to poke about in it as Simon started to speak again. But Christopher's attention was so distracted by other events in the background that he didn't even listen.

The figure who had been standing on the bump in the ground was suddenly no longer standing there but on his knees, felled by an attack from behind. As Christopher watched, he and another figure apparently wrestled. The victor in this conflict then stood up, and Christopher's heart jumped. It was a tall slim figure, who ran down the bump and towards them across the uneven ground, stumbling here and there but never falling, now and then ducking behind a scrubby bush or weaving to one side, presumably to minimise the chances of being seen. Even more amazingly, a third, large and unkempt person lumbered up to the top of the bump, stood and looked for a moment and then followed the runner, moving more slowly but making good progress. This second shape looked disconcertingly like Big Dave, except that Christopher could not remember ever having seen him run before.

'... so I'm afraid we won't be telling anyone where you are,' Simon was saying, but he suddenly noticed that he didn't have Christopher's full attention, and swung round to see what was going on in the background. He just caught a glimpse of the first running figure as it merged into another scrubby bush.

'Feroze!' he snapped. 'We've got company!'

The dark hairy man straightened up, rope in one hand and gun in the other. Christopher hadn't seen a gun in real life before, or at least not in a situation where someone was likely to use it. There were guns in museums, of course, and in gun shops, but they seemed safer in both these places - they were usually under lock and key, for a start. And they weren't in the possession of someone whom it would have been an insult to gorillas to call a gorilla. Of course it had always been on the cards, in this situation, that a gun would come into the equation somewhere. Maybe they were planning to shoot him before he went down the abandoned mineshaft, or maybe they would leave it to nature, or gravity, to take its course.

'Get him into the shaft, quickly!' said Simon. 'Give me the gun, I'll pick off the woman.'

The woman? Christopher just hoped it was Amaryllis and not Mrs Stevenson who was now racing to his rescue. He desperately wanted to warn her about the gun, but he had other things to worry about. Feroze was advancing on him, rope in hand. The mineshaft must be very close by, although it was impossible to see it if you didn't know it was there.

'Where is this shaft?' he blurted out.

'You'll see it soon enough,' grunted the dark hairy man, reaching out to take his arms.

Christopher pulled the hand that was still, unbelievably, holding the parcel, away from his captor.

'Wait a minute!' said Simon sharply. 'What's that he's carrying?'

'I thought you'd never ask,' said Christopher, wondering if the parcel would turn out to be a trump card after all. It had certainly drawn Simon's attention away from Amaryllis and Big Dave for a moment. He lifted the parcel up higher and waved it at Simon. What does it look like?'

'Jesus Christ!' said Simon. 'It's a fish supper! Of course that makes all the difference.'

Chapter 16 The Health-giving properties of fish suppers

'It isn't a real fish supper,' said Christopher. 'It's a bag of money. Lots of it. Silly money. Monopoly money.'

Very bravely or very foolishly, still brandishing the parcel of money, Christopher moved backwards, towards, he hoped, the mineshaft. He was relying on the fact that Simon and Feroze wouldn't want the money to go over the edge; they would have to stop him before he got there if they wanted it the parcel. Feroze moved in the same direction, but gingerly, as if he wasn't sure where solid ground finished and the top of the mineshaft started.

Several things happened in such quick succession that it was only because Christopher was running on adrenalin that he was able to understand and react to them.

He felt the ground start to give way under his left foot; Feroze rushed towards him and grabbed for the parcel; Christopher flung himself forwards, resisting the momentum that threatened to propel him backwards, and let the parcel fly out of his hand just as Feroze came at him from the side; Feroze got hold of the parcel, but in doing so, lost his footing and disappeared with it into the big hole that opened up in the ground beneath him. Christopher didn't see him disappear; it was just that when he struggled to his feet and looked round, Feroze wasn't there. Simon was still there, but now he was at the wrong end of the gun he had been holding. Somehow Amaryllis had reached him, disarmed him and had him at gunpoint in the time it had taken Christopher to go headlong on to the springy wet turf and Feroze to fall into the shaft.

Big Dave arrived on the scene, puffing and panting.

'What the hell's going on?' he demanded. 'Where did that other guy go?'

Christopher, shaking like a leaf now, pointed towards the hole in the ground.

'We'd better call an ambulance,' he said.

'I don't think it'll do any good,' said Big Dave, shaking his head. 'When I was a young kid one of my pals was messing about and fell into one of those things. Not here, across in West Lothian, it was, near Polkemmet. There's a country park about there now. The shafts go down a long long way. They thought they would never get him out. Only the parents insisted on it... It was filled in after that.'

Christopher shivered - or had he never stopped shivering the last time? He felt as if he had always been as cold as this, and would never get warm again.

'Dave, can you call the police and tell them where we are?' said Amaryllis calmly. 'And maybe an ambulance for Christopher? We could do with getting him checked out.'

'I'm fine,' said Christopher through chattering teeth. He was irritated to see that Simon Fairfax still regarded him with the same contemptuous smile, even though Simon was now at an obvious disadvantage.

'I think you'd better go and sit in the car with Dave,' said Amaryllis.

'No, I can't leave you here with him,' said Christopher stubbornly.

'Well, if you're going to stay here, make sure you keep out from under my feet and don't do anything to distract me,' she said with an air of authority. 'Go and sit there, under that bush.'

So Christopher's big adventure came to an end with him sitting damply and, he felt, ignominiously under a wild rose bush which gave little if any shelter from the rain, still shivering in spasms, waiting to be taken home.

Just after Dave returned from the car and reported that all the emergency services were on their way, the tall American arrived.

'I guess I'd better take my money back now,' he said, after hearing most of the story from Amaryllis as Christopher sat shivering. 'It's the property of the US government.'

'I don't think you really want to do that,' said Amaryllis.

'Why not?'

She smiled. 'It'll take a bit of excavation. And you might find out where the bodies are buried.'

'Bodies?'

With a glance back at Christopher, Amaryllis led the American over towards the mine shaft and held a whispered conversation with him. He went off, apparently in a huff, barging past the wild rose bush and sending a small shower of scented droplets over Christopher.

'Don't worry, we've seen the last of him,' said Amaryllis. 'We'll get you home as soon as the police arrive to take this low-life away.'

'And the other one,' said Big Dave, gesturing towards the other man, the one who had followed on a motorbike and who was now securely tied up with rope from Feroze's rucksack.

Home – Christopher had a sudden thought.

'You didn't leave Faisal on his own, did you?' he asked Amaryllis anxiously.

'Of course not. Jemima stayed with him.'

He wanted to ask her how the hell they had found him, but he decided not to distract her with difficult questions while she still had Simon in her sights. She certainly was focussing on him, and if looks could have killed he would have perished instantly under that frozen glare. Christopher thought it was just as well he had stayed around after all - she might have been tempted to send Simon down the mine shaft after his colleague, and then they would all have been in much more trouble.

Quite a bit later, after all the drama of the police cars, sirens screeching, tyres squealing, lights flashing, people asking questions, and ambulances, ditto, and a paramedic who was reluctant to let him go, Christopher sat in the relative safety of Amaryllis's car, being driven home. He found he didn't want to talk about anything, and that was fine with Amaryllis and Big Dave too. They had wrapped him in blankets, which Amaryllis said she always carried in the boot in case she got stranded in the middle of nowhere on a snowy nigh; but Big Dave winked at him and muttered something about being made to give up the blankets off his bed. They put him in the back seat, which was just as well since he really didn't think he could have withstood another white-knuckle ride that day. He just wanted to bask in the feeling of being safe at last, of trusting other people to take care of things for once. He knew the feeling wouldn't last long so he wanted to savour it, in silence.

The silence was broken with a vengeance once he got home. Marina and Faisal, both squeaky-voiced with relief, came rushing out of the house and clung on to him like limpets. Jemima Stevenson stood on the front doorstep and beamed widely, flashing the new false teeth she had got to celebrate her seventieth birthday or some such anniversary. Seeing the children, Christopher remembered about Caroline and the hospital roof, which minor drama now seemed lost in the mists of time, although it could have ended even more disastrously than the other incident.

He turned to Amaryllis.

'Is Caroline all right?'

He wasn't sure why he instinctively turned to her, but he had a feeling, probably illusory and dangerous, that she would know the answer.

'Sleeping,' said Amaryllis.

'Why shouldn't Mum be all right?' said Marina, suddenly suspicious.

'It's OK, Marina,' said Christopher. 'She had a bit of a funny turn earlier, which was why I had to go to Kirkcaldy in the first place, but they're looking after her now.'

That was about the full extent of what he was allowed to say for a while. Marina and Faisal ushered him carefully into the house, where they sat him down on the best chair - it had been his father's, but Christopher hardly ever got the chance to sit in it - and brought him a cup of sweetened dark brown tea. He didn't want to say to them that he had been given tea by the police, who for some reason had flasks of the stuff with them, and then by the ambulancemen (ditto) and had had enough of it. A stiff drink would have been more use, although in view of Caroline's problem he tended not to drink at home.

He sat staring into space for a while, vaguely conscious of people murmuring in the background. The word 'doctor' cropped up from time to time, mainly in the voice of Mrs Stevenson, then there was 'brandy', a recurring theme of Big Dave's, and 'work through it in his own time' from Amaryllis. He had the feeling once again that Amaryllis knew what she was talking about. He looked up at one point and caught her eye, and there was a kind of respect and understanding there that he had never seen from her before.

He must have dropped off to sleep for a while soon after that, nestled into the blanket that smelt disconcertingly of Big Dave but was oddly comforting. Later he dragged himself back to consciousness and noticed it was dark outside, but someone had left a lamp on in the room. He was grateful for that, since otherwise he might have imagined himself in the mineshaft after all.

'How are you?' said someone. He was suddenly wide awake.

'Amaryllis?'

'Yes, it's me. Do you need anything?'

'I don't think so.'

'Hot chocolate? Brandy? Toast?'

'Toast would be great.' With full consciousness Christopher tried to remember when he had last eaten. It must have been breakfast time. With an effort of will-power he started to think about the things that had happened since then. Amaryllis must have used extra-sensory perception to detect this change in his thought patterns, for she said, 'Don't try and remember everything at once. Wait till I've got the toast. Will two slices be enough?'

Sitting wrapped in the blanket, the smell of toast drifting in from the kitchen, the sound of a friendly argument between the children out in the hall, waiting for Amaryllis to come back, Christopher felt happier than he had ever done. What a pity it wouldn't last!

Chapter 17 The day after the day after....

'Toast again?' said Christopher as she brought it in. By chance she had used his father's favourite plate, a white one with a pattern of red cherries and gold flourishes.

'Of course,' she said, putting it down on the coffee table. 'Are you sure you don't want a drink?'

'Maybe later,' he said, crunching. She had waited exactly the right length of time to butter the toast, so that it was just melting in places but not dripping off the edges all down his chin. She really was too perfect to be true. Who was she anyway?

'Who are you anyway?' he mumbled through the toast.

Amaryllis sat down opposite him, on the settee where Big Dave and Mrs Stevenson had slept. Christopher no longer had a problem with that - all things considered, it was about the least weird thing that had happened lately.

'Where do you want me to start?' she asked.

'Well, for a start, how did you know where I was? Nobody saw me drive off from the hospital with the two bad guys. How did you know to come to the moor?'

'You're forgetting something, aren't you?'

'What? Did somebody call you from the hospital? The police?'

'The parcel of money,' she explained patiently. 'Remember when I got you to put the microdots in it?'

'Microdots....' He thought back to when they had been preparing the parcel, right back in the morning when they had planned to use it against the baddies in some way. Yes! Amaryllis had said she could track whoever had the parcel... so she had been able to use it to track Christopher! That part of it was suddenly crystal clear.

206

And as it became clear, the feelings he had became clear as well, and it all flooded into him at once - the fear and the panic and that sense of having been deserted by everyone. Christopher started to shiver again.

'It's all right,' said Amaryllis. 'Just wait a minute, don't think about it, and it'll be fine. Remember you're safe now.'

He took a deep breath, and found himself asking, 'So what was all this about the parcel of money anyway? What was it for? Why did the American push it through the letter-box disguised as a fish supper?'

'The fish supper was a red herring,' said Amaryllis, and burst out laughing. 'It was dirty money - it had been used for drug trafficking. The Americans got it from the Iranians – your brother-in-law in fact, or his henchmen. They tricked the Americans into being postmen for them. Told them you were a terrorist and you'd try and use the money for explosives to blow up a plane, but they were setting a trap for you to walk into - the payoff for the Americans was going to be your head on a platter.'

Christopher shuddered. Amaryllis continued.

'Your brother-in-law's friends were waiting for the parcel to get to you, then they planned to tip off the police and they would find it and arrest you... they'd be able to take the children without you getting in the way. The American bugged it so that if by some mischance the police didn't find it, you would do something silly with it, and he'd be able to keep tabs on you. Until he got the chance to - well - you know the rest.'

'Take the children? My brother-in-law's friends? It doesn't make sense – does it?' He remembered the flash of insight he had experienced on the way to Auchterderran.

He didn't really want to believe that Caroline's husband - Faisal and Marina's father - was a crook, but...

Amaryllis hesitated.

'I'll be fine,' he said. 'What has this to do with the children?'

'Everything,' said Amaryllis simply. 'Simon and his sidekick were working for the children's father, in Iran.'

'But their father's a political prisoner.....'

'No, he isn't a political prisoner. He's a drugs baron. He has so many people on his payroll that it's hard to find anybody who isn't working for him in certain areas.'

'But he can't be - Caroline said - '

Christopher ground to a halt. Caroline had let him believe the children's father was a political prisoner because he himself had guessed that was why the man was still in Iran and not in Scotland with his family. The children's father hadn't been prevented from leaving Iran by the merciless penal system; he had deliberately chosen to stay there to be in the best position to continue managing his drugs operation. No wonder Caroline was such a wreck. She must have run away from him, and been constantly worried that he would send people after her. But why hadn't she told him? And what did Amaryllis have to do with it? She was waiting now, watching him to gauge his reaction before saying any more.

'Caroline managed to get herself and the children away from him by being very brave,' said Amaryllis. 'She contacted us a few years ago, and we got her out of Iran. That was well before I retired. When it looked as if she might need protection they brought me out of retirement on a temporary basis, since I wanted to be here anyway.... I think I'm going to have to leave town, by the way. My cover's shot to pieces.'

'If it hadn't been for you, I would have been shot to pieces,' said Christopher. 'Do you still need a cover now that you've really retired? Pitkirtly's a nice quiet little place - well, apart from the things that have been happening over the past few days, that is. You could pick a worse place to retire to, all things considered.'

He didn't know why he was rambling on like this. She didn't want to hear it, and he didn't think he was making sense anyway.

'Getting back to what happened,' said Amaryllis, studiously ignoring his last couple of sentences, 'the children's father wanted to get them back, by fair means or foul. According to his value system, they belong to him - and so does Caroline. He wasn't too bothered about her though - she was no longer of much use to him. Too flaky.'

She said it without censure, just as a matter of fact. She carried straight on. 'He recruited Simon, who was one of ours.'

'A British spy?'

'We call them agents... Somebody got suspicious of him, and they decided I should come out of retirement for a while and keep an eye on things here. Simon was meant to be doing that and we wanted to give him just enough rope... His Iranian friends got a bit out of hand though - that's what all the shooting was about the other night, and the taking of Steve Paxman.'

'So it was all part of the same thing?' Christopher tried to suppress the naïve surprise that was in his mind as he spoke.

'I must be slipping – I used to be able to guess what my target was going to do, and get ahead of him, and I very nearly left it too late this time. Simon's out of circulation now, but it may not stop with him. There could be others. You have to be aware of that. But we're building up a dossier about Caroline's husband which we're going to pass on to the Iranian authorities when it's complete. He could be looking at a real jail sentence. Not a soft option, in Iran.'

'What about the Americans? Where do they fit in?'

'They – well, they haven't been very nice either. They wanted the kids too. They wanted to use them as bargaining counters. To get to their father. That was why they went along with all this stuff about terrorism – they can't really have believed that – one glance at your cv would have told them you were squeaky-clean, just an innocent playing with the big boys... They didn't want you dead though - it was Pearson McPherson who gave you the parcel of money and who rescued you from the gunman that night.'

'So this whole thing with Simon and the money and the shooting and the threats and the mineshaft - it was all to do with the kids?' said Christopher incredulously. He pictured Faisal leaning over the Monopoly board, Marina in the kitchen running her hands through the dodgy money.... he could have died because of the kids?

'Caroline and the kids can move on,' said Amaryllis, watching him closely again. 'You'd be in the clear - it's unlikely they'd send anyone after you again. Especially if you couldn't tell them where the kids were.'

'But - I wouldn't be able to see them again?'

'Just think it over,' said Amaryllis. 'Caroline isn't well enough to come out of hospital now anyway, so that gives everybody a breathing-space. She'll be well looked after - now that they know what she's likely to try and do, I don't think they'll be letting her go anywhere on her own until she's had intensive psychotherapy. And it'll take the kids' father a while to replace Simon. It's not that often one of our agents goes bad. And then they would have to plant somebody else here - I'm guessing it takes a while for people to get used to a stranger in Pitkirtly?'

'You know it does,' said Christopher with a grin, recalling the reception Amaryllis had had at the Queen of Scots that first time. He had a sudden unwelcome thought; but having had it, he couldn't suppress it. 'Where does Steve Paxman fit in? Does he fit in? Where is he?'

'Ah,' said Amaryllis. 'It was a case of mistaken identity. I believe he's in a safe house not far away, living at the expense of the British nation.'

'A safe house? What's that supposed to mean?... Mistaken identity?'

'The Iranians kidnapped him by mistake, thinking it was you. Then Simon found out and was furious with them. He knew it wasn't you and he didn't want his fingerprints found on it. He told us what had happened, in his role as one of our agents, and we worked it all out and got Steve out of the way for a while. In case he got under our feet. Which is why he's had to stay out of circulation. But don't worry, he's fine.'

'Do you mean fine in the secret agent sense, or really fine?'

'Really fine. I hope.' He couldn't see if Amaryllis had crossed her fingers behind her back. He guessed that kind of childish symbolism didn't mean much to her anyway. She continued, 'So everyone's better staying where they are for a while. Which is good for me, because I want to be here.'

'That's one thing I can't understand!' he said. 'Why would anybody want to be in Pitkirtly? Not that it isn't a nice place to live,' he added hastily. 'River frontage, harbour, nice rural area, not too far from Edinburgh and so on. People are all right once you get used to them - '

'And vice versa,' she said.

'And if you really want fun and excitement, you can always join the PLIF steering group.' A smile spread slowly over Christopher's face as he said the last sentence. 'Jock McLean's going to be so put out that he's missed it all,' he added. 'Just because of going to Milngavie.'

After that waves of exhaustion washed over him and he allowed Big Dave, who turned out to have been lurking in the kitchen refereeing the kids' arguments and probably making eyes at Mrs Stevenson, to help him to bed. It was useful having Big Dave there, since he wouldn't have wanted to ask Amaryllis to assist with that. Well, maybe later, was his last conscious thought that night.

His first thought on waking in the morning was panic.

Surely Big Dave and Mrs Stevenson wouldn't stay on now that the crisis was over?

It was much worse than that, he discovered when he went downstairs. Jock McLean and Young Dave had both appeared, somehow divining what had gone on the day before - Christopher later found out that it had all been reported on the television news. Of course there had been certain inaccuracies in the report, and Christopher's name had been given as Christian Wilsinga from Sweden rather than from Pitkirtly, while it seemed that he had been rescued from the clutches of a couple of extortionists as a result of a police intelligence operation, no mention of spies or Iranians.

'Did your department have a hand in these reports?' he asked Amaryllis, who was still hanging around too, thank goodness.

She sighed. 'No, we just left it to the news reporters to screw it up on their own. They can usually scramble things a lot more effectively than we can. They get a third-hand story from somebody who overhears the police talking in the pub, and then they make up the rest.'

'Indeed they do,' said Jock McLean ponderously. Christopher noticed he sounded more ponderous than before; perhaps he himself had now got used to being a man of action and few words, so more sensitive to wordy people. 'I remember,' continued Jock, 'when the Evening News decided to report on an incident at school. They got all the pupils' names wrong, said they had been carrying knives when one had had an air-gun, and described me as an elderly maths teacher!'

He waited for people to howl with laughter at this example of press incompetence, but for some reason there was silence around the kitchen table.

Young Dave, who was dressed for jogging, ate another piece of toast.

'Just let me know if you want to bring a case against them,' he said to Christopher. Somehow, like Jock's ponderousness, Young Dave's self-importance seemed to have been magnified by events.

'Who do you mean? The reporters? The kidnappers?' said Christopher.

'Anybody,' said Young Dave, waving his toast around so that the chunks from the extra-chunky marmalade started to fly off around the kitchen. Fortunately he himself was the only person there who was fussy enough to object to getting marmalade chunks on his clothes. He brushed a particularly large chunk fastidiously from his tracksuit top on to the kitchen floor.

'I don't think I'd go to those lengths, thanks,' said Christopher. He glanced around. 'Where's Faisal?'

'Gone to school,' said Big Dave proudly. 'The Council should give me a job as an attendance officer. I just told him he'd be in prison before he was fifteen if he didn't go, and off he went, easy peasy.'

'Yes,' said Christopher uneasily. 'Thanks for taking Marina there yesterday. The headmistress rang me up to warn me about you, by the way.'

'What?' Big Dave was scandalised. 'The nerve of it. A respectable elderly man like me! Some of those people are just too vigilant for their own good. Seeing the worst everywhere.. Well, I took Jemima along today so that headmistress can put that in her pipe and smoke it.'

Christopher decided at once not to switch on his mobile all day, to avoid having to speak to the head teacher again. Then he remembered that his mobile had been thrown out of the car somewhere en route to Auchterderran. He smiled to himself. Some good had come out of this, after all.

'Has anyone contacted the hospital this morning?' he asked, hoping that someone had so that he wouldn't have to speak to the head nurse woman again either.

There was a pause

'We didn't think they'd give information to anyone who isn't a relative,' said Mrs Stevenson in mitigation.

'You're right, they probably wouldn't,' he agreed. 'I'll ring them later.'

He got up to put more toast on, and found Mrs Stevenson in his way.

'You stay where you are, Christopher,' she said firmly. 'I'll get you anything you want.'

214

'Just coffee and toast,' he muttered. He didn't want to throw these kind people out, but he had the feeling that he would prefer to be on his own so that he could reassemble his jangled thoughts and try again to make sense of all that had happened.

The post arrived.

Young Dave brought in a letter for Christopher and then left rather abruptly. Maybe he had realised how much sugar he had consumed in the form of chunky marmalade and was going to try and work it off with extreme exercise.

'It looks kind of official,' said Jock McLean, peering at the postmark and looking on the back flap for signs of who had sent it.

'It's the Council again,' said Christopher. 'I wonder what they want this time.'

It was a massive and incomprehensible form, couched in Council-speak. Something to do with applying for funding. It rang a subdued and distant bell in his head.

'Remember,' said Amaryllis, picking up the form, 'you got a letter yesterday about this. Before – before everything kicked off. They were more or less telling you to apply. Do you need help filling it in?'

'Are you offering?'

'I certainly am,' she said. 'I want to see that village hall restored to its former - um - glory - or something.'

'Glory?' said Big Dave. 'When was it ever glorious?'

Christopher wanted to ask her about glory in the context of the tunnel, but he was reluctant to say anything about it in front of the others.

'Just a figure of speech,' murmured Amaryllis.

'If we're going to be filling in forms and that,' said Big Dave, 'we'd better get that kid Darren along to get the young person's point of view.'

Jock McLean made a hideous snuffling noise, and wrinkled up his face like a pig to go with it. 'Point of view? The young person's point of view is usually that they just want to be left alone to hang out with their pals and have a drink. Or twelve. And then maybe go and vandalise some school or old people's home. We shouldn't need to pander to that.'

'I think we'll have to, if we want the money,' Christopher pointed out. 'It's probably part of Council policy that they don't give money to anybody who doesn't press the right buttons.'

It was strange, reflected Christopher, how quickly he had slipped back into his usual routine of eating toast and having mild disagreements with Jock McLean. In some ways it was more restful than talking people down from roofs then being kidnapped and almost thrown down a disused mine shaft, and in other ways it was quite depressing to realise how little had changed. He had vaguely imagined up to now that the only reason why he lacked confidence in gatherings, and was often ignored when others were canvassing opinions, was that he was a man of intellect and not a man of action. But now that he was, unintentionally, a man of action too, it was still happening.

Christopher found himself winding down and becoming more and more monosyllabic, and somehow they all detected that he wanted to be left on his own, and they drifted off in ones and twos. Jock McLean, least sensitive person in the room as always, was the last to leave, apart from Amaryllis, who seemed to be 'minding' Christopher, either on her own behalf or that of the authorities. She wouldn't let him answer the telephone when it rang, but she did pass on a message from the nursing supervisor in the hospital, to say that Caroline was 'comfortable' and that she was now being monitored night and day to ensure that they didn't have another 'high level incident' on their hands.

'High level incident!' laughed Christopher, on the brink of hysteria. 'That's one way of looking at it!'

'Try not to get wound up about it,' Amaryllis advised. 'You'll find there isn't room in your brain to think about all that happened yesterday in one go. Better to just accept that Caroline's being taken care of now, and that yesterday is in the past.'

'So - you do trauma counselling as part of your job?' said Christopher. 'It's really a complete package, isn't it? I suppose filling in the funding application is a kind of therapy? Have you got a mole on the Council as well?'

'Certainly not!' said Amaryllis sharply, and then with a visible effort softened her tone, as if recalling that Christopher was in a vulnerable state and she should be gentle with him. 'No – I just believe in collaborating with people whose interests happen to coincide with mine.'

'Wasn't that how we got into cahoots with Stalin?' said Christopher lazily, getting up from the kitchen table and moving through to the sitting-room, where he picked up an old copy of 'Archives Unlimited', his favourite light reading.

It wasn't until the following day that he had the energy to try and find out about Amaryllis, the glory days of the village hall, and the reason she had got stuck in the tunnel. The answers were rather surprising.

'It's because of my father,' she said simply. 'He lived in Pitkirtly. Years ago, of course. He came here just before the war.'

Christopher was taken aback. He had not imagined Amaryllis would turn out to have any Scottish connections, although he had of course wondered what she was doing in such a small, relatively boring town which might have seemed to someone from the south to be in the middle of nowhere.

'Was he from around here?' he asked, afraid of pushing too hard.

She hesitated, thought about it and said, 'Not exactly.... He was a refugee at first.'

'A refugee? Before the war? Where from?... Don't answer that if you'd rather not.'

'A Jewish refugee. From Germany,' she said, apparently reluctant to tell him.

'Ah,' said Christopher, trying to sound sympathetic - not that he didn't feel genuine sympathy for somebody who had had to leave their homeland and, presumably, some of his friends and relations, behind and flee to a cold northerly climate where people might not necessarily be welcoming. 'And he ended up in Pitkirtly?'

'Yes... He settled down here and got married. Then - '

She hesitated again, and Christopher held his breath.

'- he made lots of money and wanted to give something back to the town,' she said in a final rush, apparently embarrassed.

'That's good,' said Christopher, not really understanding. 'So - what did he give back?'

'He re-built the village hall,' said Amaryllis.

'Ah,' said Christopher. Something was becoming clearer, but he still couldn't quite make out what sort of shape it had.

'The one in Merchantman Wynd. You know. The one - '

'Yes, the one where you got stuck in the tunnel behind the cupboard under the sink,' said Christopher. 'The one we went to see with Steve Paxman and the one he was in raptures over. The one that's almost a ruin again but some people think can be restored to its former glory.'

'I'm sorry I didn't tell you before,' she said. 'The old hall was a ruin - worse than it is now - people had taken away the stone to build houses so there was hardly anything left.'

'What, did he make the tunnel too?' Having previously been content to carry on not knowing anything about Amaryllis, Christopher now wanted to know everything. Or at least, everything that was relevant. He hadn't quite defined the word 'relevant' in his own mind yet.

'No, the tunnel used to belong to a gang of smugglers,' said Amaryllis, and smiled suddenly. 'My mother's family - they kept the secret to themselves for a couple of centuries. It's been handed down through the family.'

'So that's why you were checking it out the other night,' said Christopher, and felt relieved that there hadn't been any more sinister purpose behind her night-time excursion. 'Lucky it didn't fall in on you.'

'Somebody's been looking after it,' she said, but didn't say who it was. Perhaps the landlord of the Elgin Arms, he thought. He could always have used it for storage as well - maybe he even kept up the tradition and stored things he didn't want the VAT man or the Excise people to know about.

'Pity they didn't keep it free of spiders!' said Christopher.

'My father would have hated to see the hall the way it is now,' said Amaryllis wistfully. 'He always said he'd seen enough destruction for several lifetimes.'

He was still rather wary of this new softer Amaryllis, and would almost have preferred her to show her acerbic old self, at least occasionally. But no doubt that one would come rushing back from vacation if the need arose.

'So,' he said, 'what do you think are the chances of the Council paying for it to be restored?'

She frowned. 'Not that great, to be honest. It's a bit of a wreck. It was built in the early 50s when it was hard to get good building materials. Not like all those old Victorian church halls and libraries, built from stone and built to last.'

'Early 50s? So, very nearly historic, then?'

'It'll cost a fortune to restore, anyway,' said Amaryllis. 'I'm not even sure how much. I suppose part of the form is to do with getting estimates.'

'Quite a major building job,' commented Christopher. 'Maybe in the Big Society we're meant to get together, rope in local builders and structural engineers on a voluntary basis, and do it themselves, for the cost of the materials. But I can't see that happening here.'

'No, you're right. I think that sort of thing only happens on television anyway. Not in real life, where nobody does anything without being paid for it.'

She sounded wistful again, as if wishing she could be one of the people getting their hands dirty - and scratched and bruised and calloused - doing the actual work. But he couldn't imagine she would stick at it: she would get bored and feel like doing something more dangerous, or more exciting - away from Pitkirtly. He realised this was why he hadn't even tried to get any closer to her than circumstances had dictated. She wasn't meant to live out her life in a small boring place like this. She needed the bright lights, the adrenalin rush, the car chase, the hand to hand combat....

The phone rang.

Amaryllis answered it and then handed it to him.

'It's the police again. Don't let them bully you.'

'Sssh, they'll hear you,' hissed Christopher. 'Hello,' he said into the phone.

'Mr Wilson? I should just mention we have policies and safeguards in place to prevent bullying or harassment of members of the public, and we take that sort of thing very seriously indeed.'

'It's all right,' said Christopher. 'It's fine. Is this anything to do with – what happened yesterday?'

'Yesterday? No, sir, I don't know anything about that. Our investigations have been going on for some time… This is Inspector Douglas calling from Fraud.'

'Fraud?' Christopher couldn't think what he meant at first, and racked his brain to think of a place name that sounded like 'fraud' – Frood? Abroad?

'I'm afraid I need to ask you some further questions,' said Inspector Douglas. 'You may have to come over to Edinburgh.'

Amaryllis wrenched the phone out of Christopher's grasp and started to harangue the inspector. Christopher wondered if the police had safeguards and policies to protect them from people like her. It seemed unlikely. He had never met anyone at all like her before.

'... can't come over to Edinburgh! If there was any kind of communication between departments in the police, you'd know that in the past few days he's been shot at by Iranian gangsters, he's talked his sister out of a suicide attempt and he's been kidnapped and threatened, then rescued at the eleventh hour.... Well, if you must speak to him, you'll just have to come here to his house... No, of course I haven't been drinking!.. Here he is. I don't know what's so urgent about fraud anyway – that kind of case goes on for months and months.'

She handed the phone back to Christopher. Listening to her side of the conversation, he had doubted if her intervention had been at all useful, but Inspector Douglas did seem a bit on the subdued side when he spoke.

'Your – friend – has suggested we come to you, sir – in the light of recent events.'

'Yes,' said Christopher.

'It's quite pressing, so we'd like to speak to you today. What time would be convenient?'

They settled on a time later in the day. Oh, God, was Christopher's thought as he rang off, another lot of policemen for Mr Browning next-door to gawp at. There was one who should be out at an old people's bingo club to give him something to do.

At the last minute Christopher wondered if he should be more concerned about what Inspector Douglas had to say. Maybe he was too relaxed: it could be that the police were about to arrest him over the Council grant problem, about which, he now realised, he hadn't yet spoken to Young Dave. He wished he had remembered to do it earlier when Dave was merrily showering everyone with marmalade. They might have been able to straighten out the whole thing between them and avoid any fuss.

When he spoke to Inspector Douglas he realised that wouldn't have been possible. This thing was far bigger than PLIF.

'It was the bank account that made us think of you,' said Inspector Douglas. 'It had your name on it. But Mr Jackson seemed to be the one making all the deposits. Do you know anything at all about this?'

'I only found out the other day there was a bank account in the name of PLIF,' said Christopher. 'With seven hundred and eighty three pounds of Council money in it.'

Inspector Douglas and the other policeman caught each other's eyes and started laughing. Amaryllis, who had insisted on being present – 'You write down that I'm his lawyer if you like, but I'm not going anywhere' – glared at the two of them.

'Sorry, sir,' said Inspector Douglas to Christopher. 'Seven hundred – seven hundred pounds and – what did you say?'

'And eighty three,' said Christopher.

The more junior policeman gave a chortle, which he stifled almost right away.

'It's no laughing matter,' said Christopher.

'No, sir, I completely agree,' said Inspector Douglas, forcing his lips into a straight line. 'Would it surprise you to learn that the account now holds a total of two hundred and ninety thousand, eight hundred and twenty six pounds?'

'And fifty nine pence,' added the other policeman.

'I was rounding,' said Inspector Douglas.

'Yes, it would,' said Christopher, stunned.

'Would what?' said Inspector Douglas.

'It would surprise me. A lot.'

'I thought that might be the case,' said Inspector Douglas. He sighed. 'I've got to ask you this. Were you involved with Mr Jackson in setting up the account?'

'No,' said Christopher. The thought of being mixed up in something like this made him groan aloud.

'Are you all right, sir?' said Inspector Douglas, catching Amaryllis's vigilant eye.

'I'm fine. It's just so sleazy.'

'I think we're in agreement about that, Mr Wilson.' Inspector Douglas leaned forward as if he were about to get to the point of the whole conversation. 'Of course this is all confidential, but I can tell you that Mr Jackson is currently helping us with our enquiries into an important case. The PLIF bank account is of central importance.'

Christopher gulped.

'Would you like a glass of water, Mr Wilson?' said the junior policeman. 'A cup of tea?'

Christopher shook his head.

'I'll help in any way I can,' he said, finding words after a struggle. 'I didn't find out about the bank account until I spoke to someone from the Council the other day – was it Monday? Yes, I think so. Linda McSween. Department of Communities and Knowledge. I've got her phone number somewhere.'

He tried feebly to extricate himself from the nest of blankets Amaryllis had created around him before the police arrived, perhaps to emphasise her point about him not being fit to go to the police station.

'You don't need to find it just now,' she said. 'Does he?'

Fixed with another glare, Inspector Douglas had no choice but to agree.

'I thought their records must be wrong,' Christopher continued, 'but then I wondered if Young Dave – Mr Jackson – had set up the account on his own initiative to help PLIF. As a kind of surprise. But I haven't had the chance to check it out with him.'

'I don't think I'd be giving much away if I told you he was definitely acting on his own initiative, Mr Wilson,' said Inspector Douglas. 'Also for his own benefit and nobody else's. If we can get a handwriting sample from you now to compare with the signatures held on the account, that would be extremely helpful.'

Christopher's hand shook as he wrote the sample. What if his nervousness made it look, by some quirk of fate, identical to his forged signature? After the police had gone, he ran that idea past Amaryllis, and she stuck out her foot, tripped it up and then stood on it to squash it.

'Won't make any difference,' she said. 'Don't worry, you'll be in the clear and Young Dave – well let's just say politely that he'll be completely screwed. On the wrong end of the legal process. And very unpopular too – I hear the money in that account was from a pension scam.'

'How on earth did you know that?'

She shrugged her shoulders. 'Just came to me. More toast?' she offered brightly.

Chapter 18 Yet more toast under the bridge

Fundraising. They should remove the word 'fun' from it, thought Christopher gloomily as he stood by the tombola stall. So far he had sold three tickets to people who had grumbled regardless of whether they won a prize or not; he had already developed a hatred of people in general, and particularly people en masse such as you got when you organised a fund-raising table sale in aid of the Village Hall Restoration Fund (no snazzy acronyms this time). Of course, the amount of money they were likely to raise from this event was nothing, a drop in the ocean. They just had to do it to prove they were serious so that the Council and other donors would provide them with the real money that would be necessary for the project.

Christopher was surprised at how quickly PLIF had managed to organise even this tinpot event, held in the Scout Hut - a venue which didn't even live up to the level of comfort implied by its name. In his previous experience of committees, their main purpose was to debate endlessly what they were for, how they could get money from the national and local authorities to carry on with what they were doing, and who they could rope in as treasurer. But now that Amaryllis had been accepted as a bona fide member of the PLIF steering group, she seemed to have inspired them. And then there were Maisie Sue and her quilting 'girls'. Perhaps all the original PLIF stalwarts had been waiting for was a project to work on. Or perhaps they had needed Amaryllis or another outsider as a catalyst.

One thing he had never expected to see was Jock McLean dressed up as Santa Claus. Christopher had tried hard to dissuade him from this course of action.

'It's nowhere near Christmas! And I thought you didn't want to have any more to do with children.'

'I'm not entirely without Christmas spirit,' Jock had said, his words flying in the face of all available evidence. 'And people expect to see Santa Claus at this kind of thing.'

'But not in the middle of July!'

Sweltering in his fleecy suit and false beard, Jock was now dishing out presents to children in an improvised grotto constructed from a tent he had borrowed from the Scouts and decorated with cotton-wool balls.

Meanwhile Mrs Stevenson had produced a cornucopia of home-baking and presided, woolly-hatted, over her own stall. Apparently Big Dave had been up till all hours the night before icing the fairy cakes. In the corner Amaryllis ran a game involving yellow plastic ducks, an old tin bath and a couple of fishing rods.

Two PLIF steering group members were missing for reasons beyond anybody's control.

Darren had come along faithfully to all the meetings and had thrown himself into organising this event. It was just a pity that he had been arrested the day before, caught in the act of stealing three tins of Quality Street to give as raffle prizes. Christopher recalled that they had all been pleased when Darren had offered to get hold of prizes, and had taken it as a sign that his involvement in the steering group had been really beneficial.

Young Dave had sent word a couple of weeks before that he was leaving the group on the pretext of being overworked and not having time for it any more. One school of thought believed it was because he had been miffed about missing out on the excitement of the car chase and Christopher's rescue. Mrs Stevenson said she had heard at the paper shop that Dave was helping police with their enquiries into something to do with his mother-in-law's pension. Christopher and Amaryllis kept their inside knowledge to themselves.

Maisie Sue's quilting group, on the other hand, had taken over three tables, now swathed in various printed fabrics which made Christopher dizzy with their patterns – small sprigs of blossom, tiny checks, spots and stripes vied with fluffy kittens for predominance. They always had plenty of customers so Maisie Sue hadn't had time to come and bother him, fortunately. He didn't have the energy to speak to her today.

But just as the thought entered his head, she called after him, 'Christopher, come and meet Pearson!'

A tall man unfolded himself from a chair behind one of the quilt tables and came round to loom over Christopher, who said, 'I think we've met.'

Maisie Sue frowned. 'How can that be? I don't remember introducing you.'

'I didn't know who he was then,' said Christopher. He met the tall American's impassive expression with a similar one of his own. Two could play at poker. It wasn't up to him to spread doom, gloom and distrust around, especially at a Christmas Fair. It wouldn't be in the right spirit at all to break the news to Maisie Sue that not only had Pearson done something without asking her permission first, but that he had been acting as an agent of the U.S. government at the time and had since been reprimanded by the British authorities for attempting to frame Christopher as a terrorist and had been lucky not to be deported from the country. Only the fact that on another occasion he had saved Christopher's life had mitigated this. According to Amaryllis, Pearson's beige raincoat was on a very shoogly peg at the CIA.

'We met over a fish supper,' said Christopher innocently.

'That's very naughty, Pearson!' Maisie Sue scolded him. 'You know you're supposed to be keeping your cholesterol under control.'

If only she knew, thought Christopher, watching as Pearson pretended to look shame-faced. Cholesterol is the least of his worries. But it wasn't up to Christopher to enlighten her about the many lives of Pearson McPherson. He gave Pearson a manly curt nod and moved on.

Others in the town who were renowned for their involvement in various committees, community councils and church-based clubs, had rallied round and helped with the table sale; it looked as if after a shaky start the Village Hall Restoration Project did indeed have support from many sectors of Pitkirtly life. Although Christopher had been doubtful about its viability, he had to admit to having a nice warm glow at the thought of the valuable contribution he had made to such a worthy and - it now seemed - popular local cause.

'Ho ho ho!' went Jock McLean, apparently enjoying himself to the full.

'... from my granny's own recipe.... yes, butter not margarine,' said Mrs Stevenson, handing over another batch of luridly decorated small cakes.

'No - hold it this way!' said Amaryllis to a small child. 'Then you come at the duck like this - look - well done!'

Christopher smiled around at everyone.

'Wow! - a book on napkin folding - just what I've always wanted!' said the next person to win a tombola prize.

It was all coming together. The local councillor had been round, talked about 'evidence of community involvement', refused to buy a tombola ticket, declined politely to sample a fairy cake, wouldn't take part in the duck game, and glared at Santa Claus. It was all going according to plan. Christopher was sorry he had ever had doubts about any of it.

The warm glow lasted until they counted the profits at the end of the morning. All that work, and they had made exactly £63.26 (and an outdated halfpenny piece someone had put in the 'donations to the restoration fund' box).

'That isn't going to put many slates on the roof,' said Jock McLean gloomily, sitting at the end of the table in the Scout Hut kitchen, still wearing his Santa hat and red robes, but having now reverted to his normal lugubrious expression. 'It's not going to impress funding organisations either, is it?'

"It's better than nothing,' said Christopher, who felt bound to see things in a positive light to encourage the rest of the steering group and to support Amaryllis now that he knew this was her pet project. 'At least we've made a start on it.'

'But how many years will it take to raise the money at this rate?' said Jock, determined to be miserable: being Santa Claus had probably used up his entire jollity supply for at least a year.

'About two hundred,' guffawed Big Dave. 'And by that time the cost'll have gone up anyway!... Don't be such a misery, man! We're just doing this to show the council we're serious - isn't that right, Amaryllis?'

'That's the idea,' said Amaryllis.

'I wish we could go back to the way things were,' grumbled Jock. 'Going to the Queen of Scots for meetings... working through the agenda... none of this project stuff.'

'Hi there, guys!' cried Steve Paxman, bounding exuberantly into the kitchen like a semi-trained golden retriever. 'How's it going?'

His eyes gleamed, his bald head shone – Christopher was quite disappointed not to see a wet nose and wagging tail as well.

'You're OK,' he said.

'Never been better,' said Steve. 'You know what? Being away from things for a while – having time to think – it was the best thing that could have happened.'

Christopher marveled at the man's insouciance. He had been kidnapped, for goodness' sake. He had been kept locked up against his will, admittedly only in a government-sponsored safe house, but surely he must have suffered some sort of trauma or at least panic or, at the very least, resentment.

'I can't remember who it was who once said everyone should be imprisoned at least once in their life,' Steve continued. 'But he certainly got that spot-on.'

Christopher wasn't at all sure Steve had the right end of the stick about that, but he kept quiet.

'So you're fine?' said Amaryllis.

'Absolutely. I've got something to tell you all. I think you're going to be as excited as I am.'

'I doubt that very much,' said Jock McLean. He looked gloomier than ever.

'I had time to re-consider the community centre plan at length,' said Steve, ignoring Jock's input as usual.

Amaryllis looked up; Christopher saw a frown developing on her face.

'And it struck me,' said Steve, 'that community centres are a bit – well, last century. Last millennium. What we in the council want to encourage at this moment is learning. Learning for all ages. Learning and culture. Have you read our document Re-focussing the Cultural Commitment?' He glanced at the expressions on faces round the table as if searching for a sign that any of them had heard of it.

'Sounds like a good read,' said Big Dave politely.

'What are you saying?' said Amaryllis. 'Do you want us to re-build the village hall as an opera house? Is that it? Or – '

'We'd like to build on to the existing Pitkirtly library building and turn it into a cultural centre instead,' said Steve Paxman very quickly, before she could finish. He was brave as well as insouciant, Christopher reflected. He might have been well advised to leave the room immediately after speaking. Instead he stood his ground and faced Amaryllis as she got to her feet, fists clenched.

'So you're going back on your promise to help with the village hall?' she said.

'Not going back on it as such,' said Steve. 'Your village hall project has been a valuable stepping-stone to this much bigger, higher profile proposal, which I think you'll find is a much better fit to what this town needs.'

'You are going back on it. Do you think you can just divert everything to your own plans? What are you going to do with the hall? Let it fall down? Demolish it and sell the land for building?'

It seemed to Christopher that Amaryllis was about to leap across the table at Steve Paxman and attack him. He grabbed her arm and pulled her back down to sit next to him. She resisted for a moment – he could feel hard muscle under his hand – and then sat. He kept his hand on her arm just in case. It was up to him. He said quietly to Steve,

'I don't think the Council can do any of these things. In case you were forgetting, the hall and the land belong to the people of the town. It will be up to them to decide.'

Steve shrugged his shoulders. 'The lawyers can see to that.'

'Well, if you're going to fall back on lawyers....,' said Jock.

'You'll have a fight on your hands,' said Amaryllis. Christopher waited anxiously, but she restrained herself. Steve Paxman waited for a moment, then added in the same airy tone,

'Oh – and you'll be pleased to know I've talked the police into letting young Darren out of their cells.'

'No, we won't,' growled Jock.

'Yes,' Steve continued, 'I gave him a hand with his bail. I'm sure we can sort out this misunderstanding. Darren's got a great future ahead of him and I'm going to make sure nothing gets in the way of it.'

'So you're keeping an eye on him?' said Amaryllis.

'Of course, of course, part of the bail conditions.'

'So where is he then?' said Jock with an evil smirk.

Steve's smug expression wavered for a moment. He glanced round. 'He's about somewhere... Look, over there!'

They swivelled in their chairs to follow the direction of Steve's gaze. Darren stood in the doorway of the Scout hut. Christopher thought he appeared furtive, but immediately told himself off for being prejudiced.

'Come on in, Darren!' called Steve. Darren still hesitated on the threshold. 'I'd better go and get him home.

He's still very embarrassed about the Quality Street. But I know you guys will give him another chance.'

'No chance,' Jock muttered as Steve hurried away.

Amaryllis sniffed the air.

'Does anyone else smell petrol?' she asked.

'It'll be from Paxman's motorbike,' said Jock. 'The stench follows him everywhere. He pollutes the air wherever he goes.'

'You're right,' said Amaryllis. 'He takes people's ideas and twists them out of shape and calls them his own.' She banged her fist on the table. 'Damn, damn, damn!'

'Never mind, dear,' said Mrs Stevenson. 'We'll be fine as long as we stick together.'

Christopher was ashamed that the idea of the Cultural Centre actually appealed to him. There might even be a job for him there, although of course he shouldn't even be thinking like that. Certainly it would have more to offer him than a community centre. Maybe they could compromise – it might be possible to relocate the library and extend the village hall to provide something similar…

He noticed Marina and Faisal at the other end of the table, yawning. They had been very good up to now, helping here and there as the mood took them, sometimes with the duck game, sometimes with the Christmas grotto, where they had been particularly assiduous at retrieving baubles knocked off the tree by Jock's sudden hat and beard movements. He felt sorry for them, having to accompany him almost everywhere like a kind of ceremonial escort. Caroline was still in hospital, although there was talk from time to time of discharging her. He looked forward to her return and dreaded it; smaller and more vulnerable in the hospital bed, she wasn't such a scary figure as she had been in the house, and he felt sorry for her as he would have for a trapped animal, but he was only too aware that she might well revert to her old self, or worse, at any moment once she was back in familiar surroundings. He had refused an offer of counselling for himself. He didn't have time to wallow in that kind of self-pity. He would just have to get on with whatever life threw at him. Being abducted and threatened with death had made a difference to his attitude in that respect.

'OK, kids, time to go home for tea,' he said.

'Don't mind if I do!' said Mrs Stevenson brightly.

Big Dave laughed and said to her, 'You're not a kid, Jemima!'

Christopher realised that he felt an unwilling affection for all of them, even Jock McLean.

'You can all come to tea any time you like,' he said expansively, instantly regretting it. Fortunately none of them took him up on the offer apart from Amaryllis, who had planned to come with them anyway.

'We'll just leave you and Amaryllis to it,' said Big Dave.

The four of them walked along the road. The Scout Hut was in the higher part of the town, on a level with Christopher's house but in a less salubrious neighbourhood, with council and ex-council flats, and a handful of old workmen's cottages left over from the railway-building era. The sort of neighbourhood from which the clientele for youth clubs might come. Jock McLean had already pointed out that if the hall was going to be turned over to youth clubs then there was little point in renovating it, since the youths involved would almost certainly demolish it again within weeks, if not days. The others had made a silent pact to ignore him and to try and remain positive regardless of his doom-mongering. Sometimes it was difficult though.

When they heard the first fire-engine siren in the distance, Christopher automatically thought it must be heading for this part of town. He imagined either someone coming in drunk, starting a pan of chips and then falling asleep, or kids playing around by the recycling bins near the football pitch and setting fire to them just for the hell of it.

'Any news from Iran?' he said absent-mindedly to Amaryllis.

'Oh, yes, I forgot to mention it,' she said. 'They've caught your brother-in-law and locked him up. No need for any of us to re-locate after all.'

'You forgot to mention it?' said Christopher. 'You knew I was worried sick about having to move! And about not moving in time and getting kidnapped again by more goons. Why didn't you tell me?'

'I was joking about forgetting to mention it,' she said. 'I only heard this afternoon on my mobile. While Faisal and Marina were looking after the ducks.'

He remembered seeing her leave the Scout Hut for a few minutes; she must have disguised her feelings well, for he didn't think she had looked any different when she got back. But then, he wasn't good at interpreting the subtleties of people's expressions.

They saw the first fire-engine a few hundred yards away, turning down towards the harbour; a second followed it soon afterwards.

'Where are they going?' said Faisal, who had been kicking a large rusty can he had found in the gutter. Christopher worried that he would get rust on his trainers, but Amaryllis homed in on the can and grabbed it from under the boy's feet.

'The Elgin Arms?' suggested Christopher. 'Don't worry, at least they're going away from our house.'

'It wasn't Paxman's bike,' Amaryllis muttered before taking to her heels and running on ahead. Alarmed, Marina and Faisal stared after her.

'Where's she going?' said Marina. 'Isn't she coming home for tea after all?'

'Her flat's down that way,' Christopher remembered suddenly. 'She's probably gone to see if it's all right.'

'We'd better go with her,' said Marina, and started to run.

'Wait for me!' called Faisal.

'No!' shouted Christopher. 'We'll only get in the way!'

He followed them, at the more sedate pace dictated by his years and level of fitness.

As they turned the corner to go down towards the river front, there was a smell of smoke and an ominous flickering light somewhere further down the road. As they approached the corner of Merchantman Wynd, they saw the blue lights of the fire engines and, beyond them, yellow and red flames within a grey plume of smoke.

Amaryllis stood by the fire engine, gazing into the flames. A fireman tried to move her back but she didn't budge.

'Stay here,' Christopher warned the children. He advanced towards Amaryllis.

'Not so fast, sir,' said a policeman who loomed out of the smoke as it swirled round the place where the village hall had been. 'You can't go any closer than this. We'd prefer it if you moved along and let us get on with things here.'

'I just wanted to try and get this lady out of the way,' said Christopher. 'She's a friend of mine.'

Amaryllis turned and waved the petrol can at the policeman.

'Arson! That's what it is. You need to take this away and have it fingerprinted.'

He turned away, obviously reluctant to tangle with somebody in Amaryllis's mental state.

'You'll find the prints on file!' she shouted after him. 'There shouldn't be any problem matching them.'

'Just get her out of the way,' a fireman said to Christopher. 'We can't let her stand this close. She's putting herself and others in danger.'

Amaryllis wasn't listening to anything or anyone, but eventually Christopher put his arm round her shoulders and she at last consented to being led away to safety. By this time the police had got organised and were keeping all the onlookers out of Merchantman Wynd itself. The few residents who had not come out of their flats to see what was going on had been forcibly evacuated, and were milling around at the end of the road, a few of them grumbling away and others apparently enjoying the interruption to normal life.

'They should have knocked it down years ago,' was one overheard comment but on the other hand,

'They should have done something with it,' was another.

Christopher wondered who these people thought 'they' were. Amaryllis still clutched the petrol can, since nobody had agreed to take it from her as evidence.

'It was Darren,' she said. 'Never mind Paxman's bike – the smell of petrol wasn't there until Darren appeared.'

Christopher stopped in his tracks. A random memory had bobbed up to the surface of his mind and was treading water there while waving to attract his attention.

'Darren and Young Dave!' he said. 'I saw Young Dave handing over a package to Darren the other day – how much do you bet it was an advance on his wages for torching this place?... Young Dave's always said he thought the site should be redeveloped. He's maybe got a finger in that pie too.'

'He's got a lot of pies on his plate,' said Amaryllis, and suddenly shivered.

Christopher took this as a sign to lead her away up the road, followed by a subdued Marina and Faisal. Amaryllis wasn't crying, but he sensed that this might be as near as she ever came to it.

At home Amaryllis got the benefit of the routine they had developed for Christopher himself: the cosy blanket, the toast, the absorption of someone into the family circle while allowing them time to come to terms with the trauma. Christopher hoped he wasn't becoming blasé about this kind of thing. On the other hand, this time it was somebody else's trauma and not his. That made all the difference.

More time, more toast. He sat up with Amaryllis until she dropped off to sleep. Marina and Faisal had gone upstairs and put themselves to bed long before then. There was no mention of the fire on the radio news - just another little local issue, buried under the massive messy heaps of national and international news.

In the morning, she had gone. For a few minutes Christopher panicked. What if she had 'done something stupid' in the light of this latest incident? But that was just a momentary thought; reason told him that her reaction would be more likely to be something to do with revenge than self-harm. And none of this nonsense about revenge being a dish best served cold, either. Amaryllis's revenge would be swift, sudden, accurate, and as near the heat of the moment as she could manage.

He made his way to the place where he knew she would go.

The fire was out, and everything was cold. She stood by an old tree; the branches nearest the site of the building were scorched, but the tree itself didn't seem to have suffered irreversible damage.

'My father's legacy,' she said, and sniffed. He still didn't think she was crying though.

'Nothing lasts forever,' he said, not really even trying to console her but just feeling that he had to say something.

'That doesn't help,' she said.

After a while she turned away from the blackened ruins and started to walk away.

'What are we going to do now?' she said.

'That was my question!' he countered, starting to smile. He saw the faint ghost of a reflection of his smile in her eyes.

They turned the corner and walked on up the road together.

ABOUT THE AUTHOR

Cecilia Peartree is the pen-name of a writer who lives in Edinburgh. Cecilia has been writing stories since she was 6 years old, and by the time she left home to go to university she had a whole cupboard full of unfinished stories. After years of practice she succeeded in finishing novels as well as starting them.

'Crime in the Community' is the first in the Pitkirtly Mystery Series.

ABOUT PITKIRTLY

Pitkirtly is an imaginary small town on the south-west coast of Fife, not a million miles from the historic village of Culross but not nearly as picturesque. You can sometimes see the petro-chemical works at Grangemouth across the mud-flats.

The people who live in Pitkirtly are even more imaginary than the town itself, if that's possible. In a couple of cases I have borrowed scenarios from real life, but never characters. They have their own lives in my imagination.

Printed in Great Britain
by Amazon